STARGÅTE SG·1™

PERMAFROST

Sally Malcolm

FANDEMONIUM BOOKS

An original publication of Fandemonium Ltd, produced under license from MGM Consumer Products.

Fandemonium Books, PO Box 795A, Surbiton, Surrey KT5 8YB, United Kingdom
Visit our website: www.stargatenovels.com

S T A R G Å T E
S G · 1 ™

METRO-GOLDWYN-MAYER Presents
RICHARD DEAN ANDERSON
in
STARGATE SG-1™
MICHAEL SHANKS AMANDA TAPPING CHRISTOPHER JUDGE DON S. DAVIS
Executive Producers BRAD WRIGHT MICHAEL GREENBURG
RICHARD DEAN ANDERSON
Developed for Television by BRAD WRIGHT & JONATHAN GLASSNER

WWW.MGM.COM

Print ISBN: 978-1-905586-68-4   Ebook ISBN: 978-1-80070-058-1

For all our loyal readers — thank you!

Author's note: This story is set before
'The Tok'ra'(Part One)
in season two of **STARGATE SG-1**.

CHAPTER ONE

"OKAY, SO thanks for coming on such short notice." Daniel shuffled the papers in front of him, sending them skittering across the table toward the rest of the team. "Ah, I printed off copies for everyone, so you can see it for yourselves." He glanced up, adjusted his glasses. "This is what caught my attention, obviously."

"Obviously," Jack echoed, although all he could see was a picture of what appeared to be a large rock. He caught General Hammond's bemused look and lifted an eyebrow in response.

Hammond wore his amusement lightly, a slight twitch of his lips and a twinkle in his eyes. "I think you're going to need to explain that a little more fully, Dr. Jackson."

"Oh? Okay. Well, clearly it's a rune stone. But what's interesting are the runes themselves because —"

Jack held up a hand; as usual, Daniel was jumping in at the deep end. "Back up," he said. "Where did you get this?"

"The picture? It was part of a paper published in the last edition of the *Cambridge Archaeological Journal*."

"So this is on Earth?"

"Yes. It was found on a dig in Iceland this summer. That's what's interesting. Now, these runes —"

"Daniel?"

A beat of frustration. "Jack?"

"It's a week before Christmas." At Daniel's blank stare he

gestured toward Carter. "Can this wait? People have plans."

"Um, actually, I don't know." Daniel's brows beetled. "I don't know if it can wait."

"Some old scribblings on a rock? They've been there, what, a couple thousand years?"

"Three, actually." Daniel sat back in his chair, looking irritable. "If you'd actually let me talk, you'd know why that's significant."

"Three-thousand-year-old runes can't wait until after the holidays?"

"Colonel," Hammond said, "perhaps we should let Dr. Jackson tell us why he asked for this meeting."

Jack spread his hands on the table. "Yes sir." He darted a look at Carter, but she didn't appear concerned despite the fact that she was supposed to be catching a flight out of town in a couple of hours.

Daniel cleared his throat. "So — yes, Jack's right, the runes on this stone are very old. Over three thousand years old. The paper in the journal describes them as possible antecedents of the oldest known runic alphabet — Elder Futhark — but they're wrong. Well, in a sense they're right because these runes certainly predate Eldar Futhark."

"Because they're Asgard?" Carter guessed.

"Exactly."

Despite himself, Jack sat up straighter; Daniel looked a little smug and Jack guessed he'd earned the right.

"But there's more," Daniel said. "What the field archaeologists don't know is what the inscription actually says. The alphabets have diverged considerably, so their translation is only suggestive of the meaning, and they've interpreted it as a grave binding, but —"

"A what?" Carter asked. "A grave binding?"

"A kind of spell, to keep the dead where they belong."

"And?" Jack chivvied. "But? So?" These longwinded explanations drove him nuts.

"*But,*" Daniel said, returning his attention to the photo in front of him, "that's not exactly right. What it says, and I'm paraphrasing here, is 'Do not, under any circumstances, disturb this grave. If you do, you and everyone on this world will die.'"

Jack glanced at Carter — always reliable for a pragmatic response. She returned the look with a slight shrug but didn't comment.

"Okay," Jack said, thinking it through, "don't all ancient tombs have warnings like that? The whole 'Curse of the Mummy' thing?"

Daniel looked like he was trying not to roll his eyes. "Some," he agreed. "But not written by the Asgard and left on a grave that predates the Norse settlement of Iceland by thousands of years." He glanced at Hammond. "General, I think we have to take this seriously, even if there is a certain level of hyperbole in the warning."

"From what little we know, the Asgard have been pretty careful in their interventions with human populations," Carter chipped in. "It seems unlikely that they'd leave a warning without good reason."

All of which Jack, reluctantly, conceded. He glanced at Teal'c who gave a slight nod, as if anticipating what Jack was about to ask. Knowing Teal'c, that's exactly what he was doing. "Daniel," Jack said, "let me take a wild guess here: they've already dug up this site?"

Daniel shook his head. "No. That is, I don't think so. But there's a team up there right now, and they'll be working on the long barrow through the winter. So…"

He shrugged. "If it was me? I'd be in there like a shot."

"Yeah," Jack said. "So I figure someone needs to tell them to stop?"

"At least until we've had the opportunity to study the site," Daniel agreed. He ran his fingers through his hair. "General, I'd like permission to visit the dig immediately."

Hammond, as usual, had listened to everything and said little until the arguing was done. "I trust your instincts Dr. Jackson," he said. "If you think you need to be there, then I'll make it happen."

Daniel smiled, sagging slightly in relief. "Thank you, General. That's… Thank you."

Jack considered him for a moment, took in the shadows under his eyes, the tense line of his mouth. Daniel was worried and that, more than anything, meant Jack was concerned too. "I'll tag along," he said, "with your permission, sir?"

Hammond nodded. "Granted." He looked at the rest of the team. "Anyone else?"

"Sir, they don't need to —"

"I'd like to go," Carter said, before Jack could finish.

He looked at her in surprise, but her attention was fixed on Hammond.

"As would I," added Teal'c.

"Very well." Hammond got to his feet, dismissing the meeting. "I'll have Sergeant Harriman call the IDF in Keflavik and tell them to expect you."

Jack watched him leave in silence, aware of Daniel gathering his papers while Carter took her plastic coffee cup and dumped it in the trash.

"You know," Daniel said into the quiet that had fallen, "as much as I appreciate the backup, I didn't intend to get in the way of anyone's Christmas plans."

Jack stretched out his legs, easing a little stiffness in his lower back. "Nah, we'll be home in a couple days." Not that he'd had any Christmas plans for the past three years, the fact of which everyone was acutely aware. "Besides," he added, before it got awkward, "Iceland sounds like a festive kind of place. Maybe we'll see Santa."

"I think he lives in Lapland, sir," Carter said with a smile.

He tapped his nose. "That's just what they want you to believe, Captain."

Her smile turned into a brief grin, but she didn't argue the point.

"Santa Claus," Teal'c said, as Daniel finally got all his crap together and led the way back down to the control room, "is a fiction, invented for children, is he not?"

"Well, actually," Daniel said, "the origins of Santa Claus are ancient. That is, not Ancient ancient, but very old. Many societies have a similar figure at the heart of their winter solstice festivities, and, in fact, Norse mythology places Odin and Frejya…"

Jack let Daniel ramble on as he disappeared down the stairs, but he stopped Carter with a hand on her arm as she was about to follow. "Hey," he said quietly, once they were alone. "What's going on? I thought you were heading out to California tonight."

Lips tight, she made a face that said, *I don't want to talk about it.*

"Change of plans?"

A shrug. "It's complicated,sir," she said. "Family. You know?"

"Okay," he said slowly. "So you're spending Christmas where, exactly?"

Silence. She looked awkward; it *was* awkward.

"Carter?"

"Sir —"

"Swear to God, Carter, if you tell me you're spending Christmas on base..."

"Well, aren't you?" There was a note of challenge in her voice that wasn't entirely appropriate, but he cut her some slack because he knew what it was like to be alone at Christmas. Alone and pitied. The pity was the worst of it.

"Actually," he said, keeping it light, "I'm going to spend the holidays teaching Teal'c to ski."

"Really?" Her surprise was unfeigned and jolted her irritation away. "Teal'c on skis? Is that wise?"

"Probably not, but it'll be fun. And that's the point." He gestured for her to precede him down the stairs. "You should tag along."

She laughed. "I don't know, sir, it sounds dangerous."

"Well, you know me, Carter. I tweak the nose-hairs of danger, spit in the eye of stupid ideas."

"Yes sir," she said, and he could hear the smile in her voice even though he couldn't see her face. "Of course, we might end up spending the holidays in Iceland with Daniel, if things don't go according to plan."

"Oh, come on," he said, following her across the control room and down into the corridor beyond. "We're baby-sitting a couple of geeks digging up an ancient 'Do Not Enter' sign. What could possibly go wrong?"

She threw him a sideways glance. "Is that a rhetorical question, sir, or do you want me to make a list?"

The Icelandic Defence Force had been based at the Naval Air Station, Keflavik, since the early fifties, a legacy of the Cold War. Although under US Naval command, NASKEF had a small USAF contingent and as the C5 made its final approach over the bleak Icelandic landscape, Jack wasn't sorry he'd avoided being stationed there. So far. If Kinsey had his way, this was exactly the sort of nowhere in which he'd find himself until retirement.

They'd flown Space-A from RAF Lakenheath — one of Jack's old stomping grounds, back in the day — and were the only passengers on board. Turned out that Iceland, in the middle of winter, was at the top of nobody's list of vacation hotspots.

"It is growing dark," Teal'c shouted over the noise of the C5's engines. "Yet it is only two hours past noon."

"We're on the edge of the Arctic Circle," Carter said. "At this time of year, the sun only rises above the horizon for a couple hours. Further north, it never does."

Teal'c looked unimpressed.

"But you should come here in the summer," she added with a smile. "Then, it never gets dark."

"A most inhospitable region of your world. I wonder that anyone lives here."

"Oh," Daniel said from opposite them. "There are peoples who live much further north than this. The Inuit, for example."

"Are they forbidden to leave?"

Daniel laughed. "No. It's their home — their history and culture. In fact, a lot of what's generally considered 'Western' culture has its roots in Northern Europe and the extreme seasonal cycles that defined life there. You remember what I was saying about the pre-Christian solstice celebrations? Well, they originated with…"

Jack settled his ear protectors more firmly over his ears and turned to peer out the small window as the landing gear jolted into position. He had no issue with snow and ice, but the dark would be a problem. He tried to imagine living through a couple months of nothing but darkness… Yeah, been there, done that. It was enough to drive anyone crazy.

There was nothing much to see once they'd landed. A few flakes of snow fell from heavy skies, drifting past generic airport buildings that were lit up against the gloom. A plow made slow progress along the runway, adding a fine spray to the banks of snow already piled up on either side.

"Welcome to Keflavik, sir," said the chirpy young sergeant sent to greet them from the airplane. "Follow me, please."

A Pave Hawk going through pre-flight stood close to the terminal building, its engine noise drowned out by the massive C5 maneuvering toward the hangars. Jack gave the helicopter a passing glance as they hurried toward the building, his vision obscured by the low light and the hood of his parka. Difficult to fly in these conditions, he thought, worse if it was snowing. He glanced up at the cloudy sky. The last thing he wanted was to be stranded at NASKEF for a couple days before they could get out to the site.

"This way, sir," the airman said, holding open the door. "Colonel Calvin is waiting upstairs."

"Thank you," Jack said, waiting for the others to follow him inside, and for the airman to lead the way. "How long have you been in the frozen north, Sergeant?"

"Eighteen months, sir."

"Having fun?"

"Yes sir," he said, and led the way up a set of completely unremarkable stairs. "The hot springs are pretty cool."

"Kinda defeats the purpose, doesn't it?"

The kid threw him a bemused look. "Sir?"

"Never mind," Jack said, and followed the sergeant into a small office.

Lieutenant Colonel Calvin was younger than Jack and a head shorter, with an intelligent face and shoulders that spoke of too many hours in the gym on long, dark winter nights. He offered a salute, "Welcome to Keflavik, sir." He nodded at Carter, "Captain."

"Colonel," she said, snapping off a crisp salute of her own.

"This is Dr. Daniel Jackson," Jack said. "And Mr. Murray, our… associate."

Calvin's eyebrows looked like they were trying to chase his receding hairline across the top of his head as he shook hands with Teal'c, but all he said was, "Gentlemen, welcome to NASKEF." He turned back to Jack. "I have to say, Colonel, I was surprised by General Hammond's request. It's a little difficult to understand NORAD's interest in visiting the Icelandic highlands in the dead of winter."

Jack gave a dry smile. "But isn't it obvious?"

"No, sir, not really."

He leaned a little closer, lowered his voice. "We're tracking Santa."

Calvin didn't respond for a moment and from the corner of his eye Jack saw Carter swallowing a smile. But then the colonel barked a warm laugh. "I guess I asked for that."

Jack smiled too. "I promise we won't be in your hair for long." Then he winced and added, "Metaphorically speaking."

Calvin ran a hand over his thinning hair and shook his head. "I'm afraid you might be here a little longer than you think, Colonel."

"What do you mean?" Daniel said, in that way he had of seeming lost in his own thoughts and then jumping right into the middle of a conversation without warning.

"There's bad weather due to hit in the next twelve hours," Calvin said. "I've got a Hawk on standby, and if you want to head out ahead of the storm we're still within the window, but you'll be out there a few days before we can come get you." He gave a little shrug. "If I were you, I'd stay in Kef until it's blown through."

"Actually, I'd really like to get there as soon as possible," Daniel said, with a worried look at Jack.

Luckily for Daniel, Jack felt the same. If they were going to be stuck somewhere cold and dark, they might as well be doing their job, not twiddling their thumbs. "What's the flight time?" he asked Calvin.

"In today's conditions, approximately ninety minutes. Captain O'Connell is standing by."

"The people at the Kjölur site are expecting us," Daniel said. "Once we're there, we can stay a few days without a problem."

Jack gave a nod. "Thanks for your hospitality, Colonel," he said, "but we'll head out right away."

Calvin gestured to the airman waiting in the doorway. "Sergeant, tell O'Connell to expect Colonel O'Neill and his team, and escort them out once they've had time to kit up." To Jack he said, "Good luck, Colonel. Whatever it is you're looking for out there, I hope you find it."

"Thanks," Jack said. "I'm kinda hoping we find nothing at all."

Kitting up involved piling on layers of clothes, but not settling an MP5 against her tac vest, and that made Sam more than a little jittery. All she had to defend herself with was her Beretta, holstered under her parka.

Teal'c zipped up his coat, pulling the watch cap low over his forehead to hide the mark of Apophis. "I would feel more comfortable," he said, echoing Sam's thoughts, "if I were better armed."

"Yeah, me too," the colonel said, slinging his pack over one shoulder. "But we're not in Kansas anymore, Teal'c. We can't go walking around fully-armed in someone else's country."

"Why not?"

"Because… we just can't. There are rules, right Carter?"

"Yes sir. In fact, we shouldn't even be carrying a personal sidearm."

He spared her a serious look. "Oh, I think we should."

And she wasn't going to argue with that; some rules were meant to be bent.

"We don't know there'll be anything dangerous out there," Daniel said, from where he sat bundled up in his parka and waiting near the door. He looked hot, a little sweat beading on his forehead. The heating in this place was fierce. "But there had to be a reason the Asg—" He cleared his throat, lowered his voice. "That our friends left a warning behind."

"Whatever the reason," the colonel said, "let's hope it's long gone."

Sam couldn't help thinking that, if any of them really believed that, they'd still be in Colorado and not setting out for the snowbound highlands of Iceland six days before Christmas. It made her miss her MP5 even more keenly.

By the time Sam followed the rest of her team across the runway toward the Pave Hawk, its rotor blades were already turning in lazy circles. It was 1400 hours, local time, and the sun was skimming the horizon, peering out from a break in the clouds and turning the sky crimson. It would be fully dark before they reached the dig site.

"Hey," she nudged Daniel's arm, "maybe we'll see the aurora borealis."

He grinned. "That would be cool. Do you think we will?"

"Maybe." She glanced up at the sky, at the heavy cloud cover. "But not tonight."

Daniel looked up too, just as they walked beneath the chopper blades. He made a face. "You know, intellectually, I understand that this thing is perfectly safe…"

"Perfectly," Sam assured him. "We've definitely flown in things much less safe."

He gave her a sideways look. "Yet that doesn't make me feel any better."

The colonel and Teal'c had already climbed inside, and she let Daniel go first and followed him into the body of the helicopter. The pilot, Captain O'Connell, turned around in her seat and smiled when she saw Sam.

"Welcome aboard, Captain."

"Thanks." She glanced at the patch on the woman's arm. "Guardians of the North, huh?"

O'Connell grinned. "Yes ma'am, 85th Group. Guarding

the north since 1952."

Sam sat down and strapped in opposite Colonel O'Neill. "That must make us the Guardians of the Galaxy," he said, his words almost inaudible as the rotor speed started to increase.

"The what, sir?" Sam yelled over the noise.

He gave her a despairing look, settled his headphones over his ears and adjusted the mic. Sam did the same.

"You never read comic-books when you were a kid, Carter?" The colonel's words, tinny over the wires, came right into her ear.

She pulled down her own mic to reply. "No, sir. Not really a comic-book fan."

He just shook his head and waved a dismissive hand at her. "Kids today…"

Beneath her, Sam felt the helicopter get light on its skids and start to move forward. From her seat she could see out the window and watched as the lights of Keflavik fell away, her stomach swooping along with the helicopter as it took fight. Opposite, Daniel gave her a pained look and kept his eyes fixed dead ahead.

Too bad, because he was missing an incredible view. Beneath them, the setting sun drenched the snow in scarlet, jagged mountains of volcanic black pierced the ice, and all around them the sky was filled with ruddy clouds. "Wow," she breathed, pand didn't realize she'd spoken aloud until the colonel replied.

"Who knew this planet could be so awesome?"

She smiled at that, because it was true. They crossed the galaxy to visit worlds covered in nothing but pine trees, yet here on planet earth was this landscape of utterly alien beauty. "I guess sometimes you don't notice the amazing things right under your nose, sir."

A beat fell. "Nah," he said. "I notice."

There was something in his tone that made her look up, but the colonel's attention was fixed on the ground streaming past below them.

Captain O'Connell's voice crackled over her headset. "We're just leaving Keflavik, flying north-north-east into a strong headwind," she said. "ETA at Kjölur is a little past 1600 hours, so sit back, relax and enjoy the in-flight entertainment while you still can. Sun sets in approximately forty-four minutes."

Sam turned her gaze back to the window and her attention to the mission ahead. They had no idea what to expect out in this wilderness: maybe something, maybe nothing. And just like any mission through the gate, they'd be far from backup.

Danger. Beware. Do not disturb.

What would make the Asgard, of all people, leave a message like that on Earth? She looked over at Daniel, but his eyes were closed. Teal'c gazed out of the opposite window, the sunlight casting red shadows across his face.

Darkness gathered ahead, night unbroken by moon or stars. Behind them, the sun was sinking and its dying light looked less beautiful now and more ominous. It looked dark, like blood spreading across the snow.

Sam Carter didn't believe in omens. Nonetheless, she shivered and turned her head away.

CHAPTER TWO

THE OPPORTUNITY to visit other places on Earth was rare, and therefore much appreciated. However, accustomed as he was to the cold of Chulak, this dark and empty plateau would not have been Teal'c's first choice of destination.

Snow, blown up by the blades of the helicopter, swirled in the air and made it difficult for Teal'c to see the encampment only some hundred meters away. It was a low building, snow-covered yet glowing warm and golden in the darkness. It appeared most inviting and he was eager to get inside.

Colonel O'Neill, however, did not seem to share his desire for haste. He was talking with the pilot of the helicopter, his hands gesturing to compensate for the engine noise. The captain nodded, signaled 'OK' and at last O'Neill came jogging across the snow to where Teal'c stood. Daniel Jackson and Captain Carter were already heading for the cabin, accompanied by one of the two archaeologists stationed here.

"O'Connell said the storm's gonna blow through in about five hours," O'Neill said, just as the rotor blades started spinning faster, whipping up a whirlwind of snow and forcing them both to turn their backs, hunching against the force.

A moment later it subsided and the helicopter was airborne. Teal'c turned, watched it dip its nose and head back — he could only assume — the way they had come. It was too dark to make out any features, or a single star. The pilot must be flying using instruments alone.

"They'll come get us in three days," O'Neill said, also watching the lights of the helicopter disappear into the night. "But these guys have a radio, so we can check in with NASKEF as necessary. And with the SGC."

There was a tightness about O'Neill's expression that Teal'c did not like. "You are uneasy," he said, shifting his feet to keep his cooling blood moving.

O'Neill picked his pack up from the ground, dusted off the snow, and threw it over his shoulder. "You aren't?" he said.

"We have been in more hostile environments than this," Teal'c said and followed O'Neill toward the small cabin.

"Yeah, I guess. I don't know…"

"You are uneasy," Teal'c suggested, "because we face an unknown danger upon your own world."

"Maybe. Or maybe we just face a couple of sour-faced nerds and they piss me off."

Teal'c lifted an eyebrow at O'Neill's colorful language. "Dr. Gordon did not seem overly pleased to see us."

"You can say that again."

"Dr. Gordon did not seem overly —"

"Ha-ha," O'Neill said, a half-smile tugging at his mouth.

"We cannot tell him our true purpose here, therefore our intervention in his research must appear unwarranted."

"Doesn't mean he has to be an ass about it."

"Some people," Teal'c observed, slowing his pace as

they reached the door to the wooden cabin, "are born to be 'asses.'"

"Teal'c," O'Neill said, clapping him on the shoulder, "you're a philosopher."

"No more than you, my friend."

A moment's silence followed, then O'Neill took a breath and said, "Okay, let's go play with the geeks," and pushed open the door. Teal'c followed, glad at least to be out of the cold.

Inside, however, although the air was warm, the atmosphere was icy.

Captain Carter turned as soon as the door opened, her expression one of relief mixed with warning. O'Neill looked from her to where Daniel Jackson stood, arms folded, in the middle of the small area that appeared to be general living quarters. A television sat in one corner next to a shabby sofa, a large table half filled with papers dominated the other end of the room, while shelves containing books, and pieces of equipment Teal'c did not recognize, covered the walls.

At the table a man with a neat white beard and longer hair of the same shade sat rocking back in his chair: Dr. Gordon. He wore glasses, narrower than those belonging to Daniel Jackson, and a supercilious expression. "…no feasible reason why the American military, of all people, should be involved," he said, in an accent with which Teal'c was unfamiliar.

"As I explained on the phone, Dr. Gordon," Daniel said, "my research is funded by the Air Force and that's why they're here with me." He looked over his shoulder at O'Neill. "Ah, Jack," he said, "there you are."

Pushing back the hood of his coat, O'Neill deposited

his pack on the floor and took a cautious step closer. "What's going on, Daniel?"

"Ah, Dr. Gordon is unhappy about our intervention in his dig," Daniel Jackson said. "I've reassured him that we're merely here as observers, and that Edinburgh University has sanctioned our presence..."

"I don't give a rat's arse what the university sanctioned," Dr. Gordon said, letting his chair fall forward with a thud. "I want to know why the American military is interested in my excavation." He stabbed a finger at Daniel Jackson. "And you — whoever you are — can't tell me."

"Well, he *could* tell you," O'Neill said, in the casual tone he often deployed to mislead the enemy, "but then he'd have to kill you."

"Ouch," Dr. Gordon said, "be careful of that sharp wit, Colonel, you might hurt yourself."

"Yeah," O'Neill said. "I wasn't joking."

"Are you making threats now?"

"Look," Daniel Jackson intervened, before O'Neill could say more, "we're only here for a couple of days. We just want to look at your site. Once we've...assessed it, we'll be gone."

"Assessed it?" Dr. Gordon stood up. He was tall, almost as tall as Teal'c, but old and with wasted muscle. He presented no physical threat. "What on earth qualifies *you* to assess *my* excavation?"

"Yeah, Daniel," O'Neill said with a deliberate lift of his eyebrows. "What on *Earth* qualifies you to do that?"

Ignoring O'Neill, Daniel Jackson said, "How about doctorates in archaeology, anthropology, and philology?"

Dr. Gordon looked somewhat unsettled. "From which universities? Or did you buy them on the internet?"

"From UCLA and the Oriental Institute, Chicago."

His eyes narrowed. "I've never heard of you. Do you publish?"

"Okay," O'Neill interrupted, "enough of the academic pissing contest, we need to —"

Dr. Gordon spoke right over him. "What was your name again?"

Daniel Jackson appeared to hesitate, as if reluctant to answer. When he did, Dr. Gordon only huffed and said, "Nope, still never heard of you."

"Well, that's —"

His words were cut off by the door opening behind Teal'c. He turned as a swirl of icy air curled into the room, reaching automatically for his weapon. His fingers closed around air, which was fortunate because the only person entering the cabin was a younger man dressed for the snow and pulling a woolen hat from his head.

"Oh, hello," he said to Teal'c, "you must be the Americans."

Fortunately, Daniel Jackson pushed his way forward before Teal'c was required to answer. "And you must be Dr. Monroe."

"Ed," the other man said, extending a hand. He appeared friendlier than his colleague.

Daniel Jackson made the introductions again, leaving himself to last.

"Dr. Daniel Jackson?" The other man blinked for a moment, then took a step back. "Wait... oh my God, it is you."

"You know him?" Dr. Gordon appeared affronted and Teal'c felt a moment of pride in his friend; his reputation had preceded him.

"You remember the lecture," Dr. Monroe said. "The Old Kingdom and the Fourth Dynasty — how aliens built the pyramids?"

Daniel Jackson shook his head. "That wasn't the title, I —"

"Oh, surely not?" Dr. Gordon said, sounding delighted. "This is *him*?"

"Okay," Daniel Jackson said, "that was a few years ago —"

"So you recant, do you?" Dr. Gordon snorted. "Or perhaps that's why you're here? Oh, don't tell me, you think aliens constructed the Kjölur long barrow too? That is, after all, the *only* plausible explanation for evidence of Norse settlement beneath the 871 ash layer!"

He laughed again, as did Dr. Monroe, and Teal'c felt an immediate rise in tension within the room. At his side, Captain Carter's jaw was set, her weight shifting subtly forward onto the balls of her feet, as if she were preparing for action. Daniel Jackson appeared embarrassed, and although Teal'c did not fully understand the situation he understood that his friend was being mocked and was unable to defend himself.

Into the silence, O'Neill said, "So, Daniel?" He waited until Daniel Jackson's gaze met and held his own before he said, "Aliens, huh?"

"Just a wild speculation," he said, but Teal'c saw the tension in his shoulders start to ease.

"Well that's just crazy," O'Neill said. "Next you'll be telling me there're little gray men flying around up there, keeping an eye on us all."

A trace of a smile lit Daniel Jackson's eyes. "I'm not *that* crazy."

"No," O'Neill said, all humor dropped. "Remember that."

It was in moments such as this that O'Neill revealed his gift for leadership, a gift Teal'c had seen that first day, in the dungeons of Chulak; a gift on which he had bet his life, and the lives of his people.

Captain Carter shifted, settling back and away from the cusp of action. Perhaps also sensing the moment between O'Neill and Daniel Jackson was over, she turned to Dr. Monroe. "Actually," she said, drawing his attention to herself, "I'd like to take a look at the site now, before we do anything else."

There was a moment of unease, and Teal'c saw Dr. Monroe exchange a look across the room with his colleague. It was brief, but wary. He made a note to mention it to O'Neill.

"That's impossible," Dr. Gordon said, even though no one had asked his opinion on the matter.

Captain Carter looked at him. "Why?"

"I'm afraid he's right," Dr. Monroe confirmed, nodding earnestly. But Teal'c noticed that his gaze did not quite meet Captain Carter's, instead moving restlessly around the room. "There's weather closing in, we'll not be back there before daylight tomorrow."

"Back where?" Captain Carter said. "I thought we *were* there — here." She frowned. "I thought this was the dig site?"

"And that," Dr. Gordon said, "shows exactly how little you understand archeology, Miss."

She flashed him a brittle smile. "My title is Doctor Carter, sir, not 'Miss'. However, it's more correct for you to address me as Captain. And you're right, Daniel's the archeologist. My field is astrophysics."

"Well…" Dr. Gordon folded his arms across his chest and appeared to have nothing else to add.

A beat of silence fell.

Dr. Monroe cleared his throat. "Will I put the kettle on?" he said, dropping his coat onto a chair and heading for the kitchen. "I think we could all do with a cup of tea." He offered a smile to Captain Carter. "Or coffee, if you prefer, Captain?"

This time her smile was less brittle. "Thanks," she said. "That would be great."

It turned out that the dig site was about a kilometer away from the camp, which was located on what, in the summer, was the only road that ran across the country's highlands and between the Langjökull and Hofsjökull glaciers.

"At this time of year," Ed Monroe said, tapping the map with a stubby finger, "the highland roads are often closed past Hveravellir, but it's still possible to drive down to Keflavik if you're lucky with the weather and not in a hurry. But the only way to reach the dig site from here is on skis or by snowmobile. I prefer skis, for environmental reasons."

Gordon made a disdainful noise from the kitchen, which Daniel took to indicate his disapproval of 'environmental reasons'. Douglas Gordon disapproved of many things, which came as no surprise to Daniel; his reputation as an irascible, old-world elitist had been earned honestly, and he was doing a wonderful job of living up to his image.

"How long does it take to get there?" Jack said, slurping a mouthful of coffee.

"Not long, in good weather and daylight."

"Speaking of which," Jack said, pulling out a chair and taking a seat, "when does the sun rise around here?"

"Tomorrow, at 11.24."

"So there're, what, just over three hours of daylight?"

"And an extended period of twilight either side," Monroe said. "We should be able to head out by ten o'clock — weather permitting."

"Hmmm," Jack said, with a glance at the night-black windows. Outside, the wind was picking up speed and power, a few flakes of white swirling into the light cast by the cabin.

"Sir?" Sam was crouching on the floor, rummaging through her pack. "I think I'm going to turn in, with your permission?"

"Sure," Jack said, and cracked a yawn himself. Daniel followed suit. Jetlag wasn't as difficult as gatelag, but they were all tired after the long journey. The shortage of daylight wasn't helping much, either.

"Ha!" Monroe laughed. "You need to ask for permission to go to bed, do you?"

Obviously irritated, Sam sat back on her heels. "I'm on duty," she said.

"Sorry." Monroe held up a placating hand. "I don't mean to offend. It's odd, that's all, for a grown woman."

"It's military," Sam said, pulling a couple of things out of her pack and getting to her feet. She'd been given the one spare bedroom in the cabin — which even had its own bathroom — while Daniel and the others would bunk down together in the communal living area. Ed had been apologetic about the lack of space, but compared with their usual off-world accommodation, a warm, dry cabin was luxury. No one was complaining.

"I hope the wind doesn't keep you awake," Ed said, standing up from the table and walking over to Sam. "It can howl like a banshee around here."

Sam smiled at him. "I don't think anything could keep me awake tonight."

Ed nodded, patted her on the arm. "Then get to your bed." In a lower voice he added, "I hope you'll forgive my colleague. Douglas can be…challenging. He's got a brilliant mind, of course, but he's not the easiest person to live with."

"It's a not a problem," Sam said. Then she looked over at Daniel and Jack. "Goodnight, Daniel. Sir. Uh," with a glance at Teal'c, "Mr. Murray."

"Carter," Jack said with a nod, keeping his eyes on Sam — and Ed — until she'd disappeared into the short corridor that led to her room.

Daniel yawned again, and so did Jack. Teal'c, standing by the window and gazing out into the night, looked like he might have already entered a state of kel'no'reem.

"Of course, you're all jet lagged," Ed said, as if the thought had just dawned on him. "We'll leave you to rest. Doug," he said to Gordon, "let's go to the lab — I've a few things to run over with you, after today."

Gordon grunted, but didn't object. He just dumped his empty mug in the sink. "I'll be having my breakfast at six o'clock," he said, as if it were a threat.

"Don't worry about us," Daniel assured him, "you go right ahead. We're used to sleeping anywhere."

After wishing them goodnight, the pair disappeared through a door into the back of the cabin — the lab,

Daniel supposed, and their quarters — and then SG-1 were left alone.

Jack blew out a long breath, flopping back in his chair. "What a colossal pair of asses," he said.

Daniel snorted a soft laugh. He couldn't argue with that.

Turning from the window, Teal'c said, "I do not trust them, O'Neill. I believe they are hiding something."

"Like what? The good coffee?"

"I cannot say for certain. But I do not believe they have been entirely honest with us about the site they are excavating."

"Yeah," Daniel nodded, "I got that too. But you have to remember they're academics. They're afraid I'm going to come in and steal their glory; they're protecting what they've discovered. Their careers and status depend on the papers they publish."

"Unlike you," Jack said, not without sympathy.

"I *have* no academic career or status — as you saw." He looked at Jack, gave him a smile. "Thanks, by the way, for that little intervention."

Jack waved it away. "They're both morons. You know, I'm starting to hope we find some Asgard gadget that zaps them good and hard." He lifted a finger, as if coming up with a genius plan. "In fact, let's send them in first, just to see what happens."

Daniel smiled, shook his head. "Ed's not so bad. I think he likes Sam, anyway."

Jack made a gruff sound in the back of his throat and drained his mug with a grimace. "He makes terrible coffee."

He decided not to comment on the possible link

between Ed liking Sam and his inability to make coffee; he suspected the connection was only in Jack's head. "I can't think straight," was all he said out loud. "I'm gonna bed down."

It didn't take long, a well-rehearsed routine, before he, Jack and Teal'c were lying in the dark, listening to the wind howling around the cabin. It seemed to be getting louder, its strange, shrieking gusts growing stronger each time they mounted an assault. It felt a little like being under attack.

"Makes you think," Daniel said quietly, his eyes fixed on the window. Even without his glasses he could see the snow flying horizontal, caught in the wind, tumbling against the glass as if briefly trying to get in and then changing its mind.

"Makes you think what?" Jack said. He lay next to Daniel, sleeping bag pulled up to his chin. He sounded sleepy.

"What it must have been like, living here at the darkest time of the year, when all you had to keep the night at bay was the fire you kindled with your own hands."

"Makes me think it must have been cold," Jack said, his voice blurring toward sleep.

"Yeah," Daniel agreed. "Cold and frightening. Listen…" They lay in silence as the wind shrieked past. "There are several Norse myths about the creatures that prowled the night at mid-winter, on the eve of the solstice. You can see how they started, why they believed them. Imagine sitting in your longhouse, wondering, for real, whether the sun was going to rise in the morning."

"There are such myths among the Jaffa, also," Teal'c said, from where he sat cross-legged on the other side of the small living area. "It is said that, in the early days of our people, evil creatures stalked the night, feasting on human flesh. In the darkest of these times, when the day did not dawn, the sun god, Horus, was born of Isis. It was he who returned the light to the world and defeated the creatures of darkness." He exhaled a slow breath. "But that is a lie."

"It's a myth," Daniel said, "invented to explain a dark and frightening world."

"Horus was a false god."

"True," Daniel said, lowering his voice. "That is, the Goa'uld impersonating Horus was a false god. But the myth itself? That's real; that's the product of the human mind looking for patterns and explanations for things they can't possibly understand. Like why the sun grows weak, or disappears for a few months each year, like why the wind screams like some kind of murderous creature... It's fascinating, don't you think? Places like this, elemental places like this, puts you in touch with the primitive mind in ways that—"

"Daniel?"

He blinked in the darkness. "Jack?"

"My primitive mind needs sleep. So does yours."

He smiled, looking up at the slatted wooden ceiling. "Okay."

But outside, the banshee wind continued its howl and it was difficult not to imagine millennia of unquiet spirits in its voice. Daniel's smile fell away. He had always found it too easy to imagine the creatures in the dark, myth or no myth.

Laying there, watching the snow driven past the window, he understood those men who had lit fires against the darkness and prayed to their gods for the sun to rise, and for light and warmth to return to the world.

Jack woke with a start, every sense on full alert and his heart hammering. A blaze of adrenaline spread out like a flare from the center of his chest, white-hot in the blackness.

He didn't move, held himself tense and listening. The wind was battering the little hut; he could hear its joints creak, the windows rattling in their frames. He could almost feel the teeth of the wind biting through the walls, icy cold and dangerous. But that wasn't what had woken him.

Drawing his attention inside, he listened for movement within the cabin and cursed himself for not setting a watch. It was difficult to hear above the noise of the storm, but after a few thumping heartbeats he was satisfied that no one was moving inside either. He sat up, pushed his fingers through his hair, and let his heart rate slow, let his muscles relax. His watch, glowing in the dark, told him it was just after four in the morning. Not that the time made much difference when the sun didn't rise until noon.

His mind felt fuzzy, oddly disoriented. His blood was still racing, as if looking for a fight, and he couldn't just lie there in the dark. He had to do something. He had to move.

Quietly, he untangled his legs from the sleeping bag. The air was chill and he grabbed the fleece pullover he'd been using as a pillow and pulled it on, rubbing his hands over his face and trying to clear his mind. Stepping over Daniel, he made a silent circuit of the room, just to make sure there were no monsters under the bed — literally speaking.

"O'Neill," Teal'c said quietly, his eyes opening as Jack crept past him.

"It's nothing. I just…" He wasn't sure, exactly, what was bugging him.

"I sense it too," Teal'c said, rising fluidly to his feet.

"You do?"

"A sense of unease, undefined yet persistent."

Jack nodded. "You got any ideas?"

"I do not."

Jack's Beretta was sitting under his pack, loaded and with the safety on, but he resisted the urge to fetch it. Unless the two history geeks had gone psycho, there was no apparent danger here beyond the storm, and a pistol wasn't going help calm the wind. And yet… Something was making the hairs rise on the back of his neck and he'd learned a long time ago not to ignore his instincts.

"Go check on Carter," he told Teal'c, because a little paranoia never hurt anyone.

As Teal'c silently left the room, Jack approached the window with a trepidation he didn't fully understand. Outside, the night was raw and black. No moon, no stars, no light at all. Daniel was right; places like this brought you right back to basics, back to monsters hiding in the shadows.

Lifting a hand, he pressed it to the window. It was icy under his fingertips, his breath misting against the glass as he watched the snow fall. He could feel the cabin shake as each gust slammed, broadside, into the frame. He hoped Icelandic builders knew what they were doing and glanced up at the ceiling, just in case.

And when he looked back out at the storm, something was moving in the dark.

His heart skipped several beats; the breath froze in his chest.

There was something out there, a shadow against shadows, heading into the wind. He could see the snow eddying around it in swirls. Mouth dry, he worked his jaw to speak. "Daniel?" It was no more than a rasp. He turned, hissed louder. "Daniel!"

"Huh?" Daniel sat bolt upright, grasping for his glasses. "What…?"

"There's something out there."

He turned back to the window, but he'd lost it — the shape was gone. All he could see now was snow. "Damn it."

Daniel scrambled to his feet and came to join him. "What was it?"

"I don't know. An animal, maybe?" But it hadn't looked like an animal; it had looked human.

Behind them, a light came on. "Everyone okay?" Monroe shuffled drowsily into the room.

"Yeah, sorry to wake you," Daniel said. "We — It looked like there was something outside."

Monroe scrubbed a hand through his hair. "That's not possible."

"An animal, maybe?"

He shook his head. "There's precious little wildlife up here in the winter. An arctic fox, maybe, nothing bigger."

"No bears?" Jack said. It could have been a bear, maybe, with that upright shambling gait.

"No bears in Iceland," Monroe said, "except the occasional stranded polar bear."

"What about a person?"

"A person? There's no one for miles around — your eyes were playing tricks, Colonel. It's a dark night."

Maybe, Jack thought. Maybe not. The light from the corridor had turned the glass black; all he could see now was his own disheveled face staring back at him.

"Monsters in the dark," Daniel said, pulling off his glasses and rubbing his eyes.

"Aye," Monroe nodded. "*Daugr* and *haugbui* — you're not the first man to imagine monstrous beasts in the wild places of the north."

In the window's reflection Jack saw Daniel move closer and their gaze met in the glass. Jack didn't believe in magic and, although he knew his eyes were quite capable of playing tricks, he was pretty certain that he'd seen *something* out in the storm.

And he was pretty certain that Daniel believed him; they both knew monstrous beasts were real, after all.

CHAPTER THREE

"SIERRA Golf Charlie this is Sierra Golf One Niner." The colonel sat at the radio set in the far corner of the room, legs stretched out and one eye on the archeologists arguing *sotto vocce* in the kitchen. He looked relaxed, but Sam knew he was anything but. "Sierra Golf Charlie, this is Sierra Golf One Niner."

The radio hissed and at last Harriman's faint voice crackled out of the speaker. *"Sierra Golf Charlie, send."*

"One Niner, we're at base camp one klick due south of the site. Holed up in bad weather over night. Clearing now and moving out to take a visual recon in thirty minutes. Will advise the outcome in twelve hours. Over."

"Charlie, solid copy. Have fun in the snow. Out."

The colonel cocked an eyebrow at the snow comment. "Easy for him to say."

Sam smiled and pushed her foot into her boot. Through the window, dawn was breaking along the horizon. It wasn't snowing anymore, but the sky was still heavy with clouds and it almost seemed as though the sun was slipping in beneath them, its light sliding horizontally over the snowy planes of the earth.

"...well you'll have to. We have no *choice!*" Ed Monroe's voice rose from the kitchen in evident exasperation. He'd been arguing with the obstreperous Dr. Gordon all morning, presumably trying to make his colleague see sense.

Perhaps feeling her eyes on him, Monroe turned and offered Sam a smile that was more nervous than apologetic. It made her think that Teal'c was right; these two were hiding something. She just hoped it was all to do with professional jealousy and nothing to do with Asgard technology.

"I maintain it's ridiculous," Gordon said, addressing Monroe although his words were loud and obviously meant for them all. "The American army has no right to be here. They can't just march all over the world as if they own it!"

The colonel bristled but didn't rise to the obvious bait. He just pushed his hands through his hair, took a breath, and stood up. "Okay," he said, like a camp leader rallying his troops, "get your skis on kids, we're moving out."

"You can't give me orders," Gordon protested. Unlike the colonel, he *was* rising to the bait.

"Nope," O'Neill said. "You can stay here and polish your fossils, if you like. But my team is going to do what we came here for. Daniel…" He glanced around. "Where is he?"

"He is still in the laboratory," Teal'c said. He was already kitted out in cold weather gear, although he'd refused skis and said he would run alongside them. Sam didn't doubt he could do it.

"Daniel!" the colonel yelled, making Gordon jump so hard he knocked over his coffee mug on the kitchen counter.

"For goodness' sake!"

The colonel just shrugged.

And then Daniel popped his head around the door

that led to what was, generously in Sam's opinion, designated as the 'lab'. "You bellowed?"

"We're heading out," the colonel said. "Get your stuff."

"Oh. Okay, I was just —"

"Daniel? Daylight, remember?"

Daniel looked at the window, blinked, and said, "Yes, yes right. Sorry. I'll be right with you."

Inevitably, Daniel's idea of 'right with you' didn't tally with the colonel's, but eventually — after about thirty minutes — they were all ready to go. Gordon, bundled up in a red snow suit, took one of the snowmobiles while Monroe offered to guide SG-1 on skis. Teal'c's decision to run drew a skeptical look from Monroe, but no comment. He was smarter than his colleague, Sam figured.

"Don't touch anything until I get there," Daniel warned Gordon. "It's important."

It was difficult to see Gordon's expression beneath his reflective sunglasses, but his tone of voice was clear enough. "It's *my* site, Dr. Jackson. You're here under sufferance."

With that, he kicked his snowmobile into life and started out cautiously across the new snow.

Monroe watched him go with a tense expression, then cast a worried glance in Daniel's direction. Sam didn't think Daniel noticed it, but she did.

"Problem?" she said, maneuvering herself toward Monroe. It had been years since she'd skied cross country and it was taking her muscle memory a few moments to kick in.

Monroe just shook his head. "No, it's just…this is a big find, you see. Huge." He glanced at Daniel again. "Things like this make or break careers. We have to be cautious."

"Daniel has no intention of stealing your find," she assured him. "Or taking the credit. Quite the opposite, in fact."

"Really? So why is he here? Why is he here with you? None of it makes much sense."

"No," she agreed, flicking a glance at the colonel as he gave the signal to move out. She adjusted her sunglasses, pushed off with her ski poles. "Let's hope it stays that way."

It was actually pretty amazing, skiing across the snowfield with the low sun slanting in from the east. The colonel kept the pace reasonable, because it wasn't far and it was clear that Monroe didn't share their level of fitness. Teal'c, on the other hand, didn't even break a sweat running alongside.

But it was a quiet half hour and gave Sam time to think. It would be Christmas in just five days, and here she was in the far north of the world instead of at home with family. And no one was missing her. She hadn't seen her dad for years and as for Mark… The truth was, she didn't have a family — not really, not anymore. Perhaps she hadn't since the day she'd lost her mom. And most of the time it didn't matter; most of the time her life was amazing. But sometimes, especially during the holidays, she felt an absence somewhere inside, a hole she couldn't fill. And sometimes, as astonishing as her life was, she longed for that sense of belonging she'd lost.

"What's on your mind, Carter?" the colonel said, startling her. She hadn't notice him drop back to her side.

She shook her head, glanced over at him. How could she talk to him, of all people, about lost families? "Just trying to figure out what's going on here, sir," she said instead.

"Nothing, I hope."

"Yeah."

He frowned, kept his eyes straight ahead, and said, "Listen, I think I saw something last night, out in the storm."

"Really?" His obvious unease spiked a beat of alarm. "What kind of something?"

"I don't know. Something moving."

"An animal?"

He shrugged. "Just keep your eyes open."

"Yes sir."

He gestured ahead. "Looks like we're almost there."

A long, low structure — like a barn — was coming into view. It was probably thirty meters long, single-story, its wood glowing gold in the sunlight.

"Wow," Daniel said from up ahead. He was talking to Monroe. "You built a shelter over the whole long barrow."

Monroe nodded. "It's the only way to keep working on the site through the winter, and it's a significant enough find to make that necessary."

"I'm looking forward to seeing it."

A silent beat fell. "I'm sure you'll find it impressive," Monroe said at last.

"How close are you to getting inside the actual burial chamber?"

Monroe didn't answer that, lifting a hand instead to wave at Dr. Gordon who was just emerging from the building. His snow mobile was parked off to the side. "Everything okay, Doug?"

"No," the other man called back, stomping through the snow to meet them. "The damn door blew open in the night."

"What?" Monroe started forward.

"You can't have shut it properly."

"Of course I shut it!" He looked at the door, then back at Gordon. "Was anything damaged?"

"The generator stalled," Gordon said, "but I restarted it. Luckily, it seems okay." He shoved his hood back. "But you need to be more careful."

"I shut the bloody door," Monroe insisted, but only beneath his breath. "Look, let's just get on with this shall we?"

"By all means." Gordon gave Daniel a scathing look. "Let the inspection begin."

"It's not —" Daniel said, then clearly changed his mind. "Just show me what you've found and we'll take it from there."

Inside the shelter, it was pretty basic. The small generator that provided power for lighting and heating had a snowdrift piled up against it, melting now that it was running again, and a crude bench was fixed to the walls closest to the doors. Past that stood the black entrance to the long barrow — a narrow hole carved into a low mound, no more than two feet high.

"Most of the barrow is underground," Monroe explained, "which is interesting in itself. It was excavated into the ground, dug into the permafrost itself."

"Most long barrows," Daniel explained, for the benefit of the rest of them, "are constructed above ground level."

"Like pyramids," Gordon said. "Except without any alien involvement, naturally."

Daniel gave a tight smile and said, "When you say 'most of the barrow' is below ground, how much of it — exactly — have you excavated so far?"

Gordon looked bullish, Monroe uneasy. Neither of them answered.

"Oh for crying out loud," the colonel said, "you already opened it, didn't you?"

"And why not?" Gordon protested. "This is my find, my discovery!"

"It was *our* find," Monroe corrected, but his voice was quiet, almost as if he didn't want to be heard. He wasn't.

"I'm not about to let some crackpot peddler of the ridiculous take the credit for the find of the century," Gordon carried on. "Of course I opened the burial chamber. You were a fool if you thought I wouldn't."

Daniel's eyebrows shot up almost as fast as the colonel's slammed down into a scowl. "Do you have *any* idea what could be down there?" he snapped.

"Yes I do," Gordon retorted. "One of the greatest discoveries in modern archeology."

"Or one of —"

Daniel put a placating hand on the colonel's arm. "I think," he said to Monroe, "we just need to go down and take a look."

Monroe glanced at his colleague. "Go ahead," Gordon said, "play tour guide. I'll start shoveling the snow before it melts all over the floor."

Ignoring the jibe, Monroe turned back to Daniel. "The permafrost has resulted in an incredible level of preservation. I think you'll be impressed."

"Oh, I already am," the colonel growled, yanking his arm away from Daniel. He looked like he didn't know what to do with his hands, like he was looking for a weapon that wasn't there. Sam knew how he felt. "These are *really* impressive levels of stupidity."

Monroe frowned and Sam couldn't really blame him. He couldn't possibly have any idea of the potential dangers. "I'll grab a couple of torches," Monroe said, and headed over to the workbench.

"Sir," she said as they waited, "you know he can't really imagine—"

"He can follow orders."

Her doubt must have shown on her face because, after a pause, the colonel sighed and added, "Or not, I guess. What is it with archeologists and their inability to follow orders?"

"It's because we're naturally independent, inquisitive thinkers," Daniel said.

"Yeah? I thought you were just natural pains in the ass."

He shrugged. "That too."

Sam was a little disappointed that the torches Monroe returned with weren't the flaming variety, but instead heavy duty flashlights. He handed one to her and one to the colonel. "Follow me."

She glanced at O'Neill. He'd undone his parka, giving him faster access to his sidearm, although he hadn't drawn it yet. She did the same.

"Let's go," the colonel said with a nod to the rest of the team. Together, they followed Monroe down into the burial mound.

It was cold, dank and musty. The passageway was cramped and Sam felt her shoulders brushing each side of the wall as she followed Teal'c, bringing up the rear. Ahead of her, the light from Monroe's flashlight flitted ahead of them, bouncing off wooden supports holding up the structure.

"You're sure this place is sound?" the colonel said, glancing upward.

"It's lasted for three thousand years," Monroe called back, his voice deadened in the cramped space.

That wasn't entirely reassuring, but then again they'd been in worse places.

"In terms of grave goods," Daniel said from somewhere between Teal'c and the colonel, "what did you find?"

There was a hesitation before Monroe said, "Very little beyond the rune stone." He'd stopped now and Sam peered past Teal'c to glimpse another, narrower, opening. "We were initially disappointed, until we found this chamber."

"What's in there?" the colonel said. They were standing close together in the cramped space and she could see his breath misting in the freezing air. Short sharp breaths; he was nervous. She felt a little creeped out herself. Glancing back the way they'd come, she could see the light filtering down from the shelter above them. All it would take was for someone to fill that hole in…

The colonel shifted, his arm brushing hers, and her attention returned to Monroe. His face was almost monochrome in the shifting shadows cast by the flashlights. "In there, Colonel O'Neill," he said, "is the burial chamber itself. And, like I said before, there's a remarkable degree of preservation."

He looked at them for a moment, as if expecting the prospect of encountering a three-thousand-year-old corpse to spook them. When nobody reacted he gave a half shrug and said, "I'll go first. One at a time through the doorway — we only opened it yesterday and haven't had time to reinforce it."

They hadn't done a very neat job of it, either, Sam thought as she waited for Teal'c to squeeze himself sideways through the opening. It looked like they'd just burrowed their way through with bare hands; she could still see finger marks around the doorway.

The chamber was obviously larger than the passageway. She felt its size even if she couldn't see it at first. The air was dryer too, if not warmer, and there was rock and not earth beneath her feet; she could hear the scuff of their boots against it.

"You can see inscriptions on these columns," Monroe was saying, his flashlight darting over to the sides of the chamber. Sam turned her own beam in the same direction, illuminating stone pillars that ran from the ceiling to the floor, all covered in runes.

"Look familiar?" the colonel asked Daniel.

He just nodded, his glasses glinting in the erratic light.

"We can't translate it," Monroe said, "which is very exciting. This actually predates all known runic alphabets. It could be the root of the written Norse language and we have no idea how it got here or who put it here."

"Exciting," the colonel said, in a tone that implied the opposite. He nudged Daniel, lifted an eyebrow. *Well?*

Daniel gave a helpless shrug. "I'll need to transcribe it," he said out loud. Then, with a wary glance at Monroe, "It looks like it could be a history of the people who built this place."

The colonel just nodded, thoughtful.

"And over here," Monroe carried on, ski boots clicking across the stone floor as he reached the back of the chamber, "is the *pièce de résistance*. This is the reason we're so phenomenally excited about —"

He stopped dead.

Sam turned, caught the stricken look on his face. "What?"

In front of him the chamber curved up, like the walls of a cave that had been sandpapered smooth. They glistened in the flashlights beams and she saw symbols written there that were recognizably Asgard, the kind of thing you might see on one of their ships. She could almost smell their technology.

In front of the wall (or was it a control panel?) sat a long stone table, about knee height, which was also polished to a shine. Monroe was staring at it in utter disbelief.

"Monroe?" the colonel said when the silence stretched too long. "Something wrong?"

The archaeologist's lips moved, his head shook, and he swung his flashlight around the room as if searching for something. "It's impossible," he said. "I don't understand."

"What?" the colonel said tensely.

Sam felt her muscles tighten. Behind her Teal'c took a breath, drew half a step closer.

"Dr. Monroe?" Daniel prompted.

Monroe whirled back to face them, shading his eyes from the glare of the colonel's flashlight. "It's gone," he said. "It was here, and it's gone."

"What's gone?"

"The body," Daniel guessed. "There was a body here, right, and now it's gone?"

Monroe nodded. "I don't understand. Who would have taken it?"

The colonel must have drawn his weapon because Sam heard him chamber a round. "Are you sure it was dead?" he said.

"What?" Monroe looked at him like he was crazy. "It was three thousand years old. A three-thousand-year-old Norse warrior king! Of course it was dead."

The colonel didn't answer that. "Carter," he said, "Teal'c, take a look around."

"Yes sir."

"This is insane," Monroe said, as Sam made her way over to the wall behind the empty dais. "Someone must have taken it."

"Yeah?" O'Neill said. "Who? Your buddy upstairs?"

Monroe shook his head. "Why would he? We haven't even catalogued or photographed the find properly. Moving it would do tremendous damage to the integrity of the site. Doug knows that."

Sam ran her fingers over the smooth walls, tracing the writing. It was definitely Asgard technology, but there was no power. Whatever this was designed to do, it was as dead and cold as the rest of the grave. Turning, she crouched next to the dais. There was a small hexagonal depression, about the size of a baseball, at one end which looked like it was designed to hold something, but she'd need more time to study it before she could figure out exactly what.

"O'Neill," Teal'c said then. He was standing next to the narrow opening, examining the fingerprints in the dirt walls. "Someone has passed through here, something larger than either Dr. Gordon or Dr. Monroe."

"You?" the colonel asked, and only half facetiously.

"The thief," Monroe said. "The grave robber, it must be."

Daniel cleared his throat. "Well — however it left here — we need to find it."

"And we need to lock down this site," the colonel said.

Monroe stared at him, eyes wide. "You can't. Doug would never permit —" His expression turned bleak. "Oh God, I have to tell Doug. Excuse me."

Pushing past Teal'c, Monroe slid back into the passageway.

"I'll go with him," Daniel offered. "Make sure they don't do anything stupid."

Sam watched him go, and then turned to Teal'c. "A Goa'uld is the obvious explanation," she said in a low voice. "But I don't sense anything. Do you?"

"I do not," Teal'c said, crossing the chamber toward them. "If it was a Goa'uld, they are long gone from this place." He looked at the colonel. "The figure you saw in the storm last night? A human could not survive unprotected in such weather, but a Goa'uld could."

O'Neill nodded. "My thoughts exactly." He took a breath, made a decision. "We'll head back to base camp and contact the SGC. Looks like we're gonna need backup after all."

The term FUBAR was circling in Jack's mind as he held down the talk button on the cabin's long-wave radio. "Sierra Golf Charlie this is Sierra Golf One Niner, over."

Nothing came back but static.

"Sierra Golf Charlie this is Sierra Golf One Niner, over."

Still nothing.

"This is absolutely preposterous!" Gordon hadn't taken the news of the missing body well, and was storming about in the middle of the living area like a wrathful old hippie. "You!" he said, stabbing a bony finger at Daniel. "You must have engineered this. How else could it possibly have happened?"

Jack ignored him, pressed the talk button again. "Sierra Golf Charlie this is Sierra Golf One Niner, over."

"Look," Daniel said, hands up. "I understand how strange this must seem to you, but —"

"Don't give me platitudes. Do you think I'm a fool? You've stolen this discovery right out from under my nose. And, given your disreputable credentials, I can't say I'm surprised."

Jack decided to change tack. "IDC Keflavik this is Colonel Jack O'Neill, over."

Still nothing but dead air.

Carter was watching him from the other side of the room. "Maybe the antenna's down, sir? I could go out and take a look."

"Are you kidding?" The snow had started falling even before they'd gotten back to the cabin, cutting short the sorry excuse for a day. And it was howling past the windows now, whipped along by the north wind. "You can check it in the morning — if we get one."

"But what about backup?"

He shook his head, shut down the radio. "No one's flying in this anyway," he said. "We'll just have to wait it out."

She darted a look at Gordon, who'd retreated, fuming, to the kitchen, banging around pots and pans. "It's going to be a long night, sir."

"Yeah." And because he couldn't put it off any longer, he got to his feet. "Okay, look," he said to the room in general, but mostly to Gordon and Monroe. "Something hinky's going on here. We don't know what, exactly, but at the very least there's a crazy guy out there with a fetish for dead old men."

Daniel raised his eyebrows, but Jack ignored him. Gordon, on the other hand, was turning puce. Jack stalled an outburst with a raised hand. "Point is, we need to be on our guard tonight. And we don't need to be fighting among ourselves." He looked directly at the archeologist. "And that means you, Indiana."

"You've got a bloody cheek," Gordon snarled. "How dare you give me orders? You think you can just swan in to any —"

"Look," Jack growled, his temper starting to fray, "you have no idea what's happening here. So you'll do as you're told or, so help me, I will tie you to a damn chair until we're done. Because I will not let you jeopardize the lives of my team. Do you understand?"

"I won't —"

"*Do you understand?*" It was the kind of bark that he rarely used and he saw Carter tense, giving him an uneasy glance.

Gordon's lips clamped shut, rebellious but, thankfully, silent.

"Good," Jack said, forcing himself to take a breath and relax. He'd been on edge since they got here and the missing dead guy wasn't helping. "So we're gonna eat, then we're gonna sleep." He looked at his team. "I'll take the first watch, then Teal'c, Daniel and Carter."

"Watches?" Monroe said. "You really think that's necessary, Colonel?"

"Well we're not doing it for fun."

They ate mostly in silence. Gordon took his meal into the lab and ate alone, while the rest of them sat hunched around the table, periodically glancing out the window as sudden gusts slammed into the cabin.

No one seemed particularly hungry, and not just because of the unappetizing rehydrated food. *Worse than MREs*, Daniel thought, prodding the rice and bean mixture around his plate.

Sam mentioned it first, though, the weird kind of white-noise tension in the back of her head. "It's like interference," she said, pressing her fingertips against her neck, "like it's making it hard to think."

"I thought it was just me," Jack said, pushing his half-empty plate away. "But then thinking's never been my forte."

Sam gave a listless smile, but didn't reply.

"I've had a headache all day," Monroe joined in. "I think it's from the storm, changes in atmospheric pressure or something."

Sam made a face, as if she thought that was stupid but was too polite to argue.

"How about you, big guy?" Jack asked Teal'c. "You feeling anything unusual?"

"I am. More than I would expect." It was all he could say with Monroe right there, but they all knew the subtext; Teal'c was often protected by his symbiote. It didn't always mean anything when he wasn't, but sometimes it did.

Despite the fuzz in his head, Daniel was still thinking. He'd been considering the snatches of Asgard text he'd managed to read in the long barrow. There hadn't been time to transcribe any before the disappearance of the body had been discovered, but it had been clear to him that what had been written on the walls of the burial chamber hadn't been written by the Asgard. That is, it had been written using Asgard script but the words, the context, had been born of human minds, not an advanced alien species.

He glanced at Monroe, who sat toying with his food. Unable to reveal how much of the language he knew — it would be impossible to explain — Daniel decided to approach the subject obliquely. "Norse mythology," he said, "often refers to undead creatures called *draugr*."

That got Jack's attention. He looked up and Daniel tried to convey, with a look, that what he was about to say had been written on the walls of the long barrow. "I read recently that their proximity alone can drive people mad with fear."

Jack glanced over at Teal'c and Carter. They were both listening too.

"You're not suggesting there's a *draugr* out there, are you, Dr. Jackson?" Monroe said with a tired laugh. "That's as farfetched as little green men."

Daniel spared him a tense smile. "I'm not suggesting anything. But you're familiar with the mythology, right?"

"Of course. And I suppose ancient humans were as prone to mental illness, or to the effects of changes in atmospheric pressure, as we are. Mythology is simply a narrative explanation for the unknown."

Jack nudged Daniel's arm, getting his attention. "Anything else you've read recently that we should know about?"

"Um…" He considered how to phrase it. "Well, apparently *draugr* are difficult to kill. The gods were deemed necessary to bind them inside their graves."

"Oh, not always," Monroe objected. "What about Glámr? He was killed by Grettir." He looked at Jack.

"Grettir was a human," he clarified. "Not a god."

Daniel scratched his head. "But what about the Wild Hunt?" Another glance at Jack. "Odin — one of the Asgard pantheon of gods — hunts down *draugr* and other supernatural creatures. On the eve of the winter solstice, actually. Which is two days from now."

"That's just one of many iterations of the myth," Monroe said. "Although Dr. Jackson's right about the link with mid-winter; the *draugr* Glámr, of course, rose from the dead on Christmas Eve." He gestured with his fork at the windows and the wind-driven snow. "In some parts of the world, the Wild Hunt was said to ride on the north wind. You can understand why, yes?"

"Is there any evidence," Sam said carefully, "of what the *draugr* might have actually been?"

Monroe just laughed. "They weren't actually anything, Captain. They were shadows in the night. Fairy tales." He sat back in his chair, regarding Daniel with a curious expression. "Myths are no more than stories, Dr. Jackson. Perhaps that's where your academic career took such a wrong turn." His tone wasn't unkind, but it was condescending and Daniel felt his hackles rise. "Mankind is capable of great self-deception," Monroe carried on. "Just because our ancestors believed that the gods flew across the skies in chariots of fire, it doesn't mean they were right." He paused. "It doesn't mean that alien intelligence was responsible for the great works of the past."

"No one's talking about aliens," Jack grumbled.

Although, Daniel thought, they probably were. A Goa'uld, perhaps, would have seemed like a creature that rose from the dead to harry the terrified human population. A Goa'uld might have been something the

Asgard stepped in to control. "What I think," he said to Monroe, "is that, in any given situation, we all hold part of the truth. And anyone who thinks he has it all is probably wrong."

Monroe didn't try to argue with that.

Daniel slept heavily, like he was sinking into a thick, boggy darkness, and it was difficult to rise to the surface when Teal'c woke him for his watch.

"You are weary," Teal'c whispered, crouching next to him in the dark. "I will take your watch."

"No, don't. I'm good." He rubbed his hands across his face, reached for his glasses. His brain felt stuffed full of cotton, but it was probably nothing coffee wouldn't cure. "You need to rest too."

Teal'c inclined his head. "I do feel the need for rest," he agreed. "Unusually so."

"Atmospheric pressure?" Daniel suggested with a wry look.

"I do not believe so. My symbiote is disturbed."

"Yeah," Daniel said. "I know how it feels."

There was still coffee in the pot, and Daniel poured himself a cup. It was stewed, but all he really needed was the caffeine and he didn't want to wake the others by making a new pot; they were all bunking in the living area tonight, on Jack's orders — all except Gordon, naturally. But even the coffee couldn't penetrate the fuzzy-headed feeling with which he'd gone to bed, the feeling that had intensified during the night into a crawling, disturbing unease. Like cold fingers down his spine, like spiders spinning cobwebs in his brain.

He shuddered, scrubbed a hand through his hair, but failed to shake it off.

"Focus on something else," he told himself.

Outside, the storm had abated. The snow was still falling, but at least it was more vertical than horizontal. He guessed that was an improvement and got a little closer to the window, trying to make out the shapes of the tarpaulin-covered snowmobiles outside. But the external lights were out, he realized with a beat of unease, and he couldn't see anything beyond the window.

And his chest felt tight suddenly, as if a hand was squeezing his lungs so he couldn't suck in a whole breath. He tried to swallow and couldn't. In his hand, the coffee mug started to shake and he set it down clumsily on the counter.

Panic attack.

He'd never had one before, but this must be how they felt: frozen, rooted to the floor, short gasping breaths, muscles like iron, mouth dry. All he could do was stare out into the snow, leaning closer to the window as if drawn toward it. Cold radiated from the glass, he could feel it against his eyes, his breath was misting the glass as he leaned closer and —

There was a face at the window.

"Argh!" Daniel stumbled backward, the mug smashing on the floor.

Dead eyes stared at him through tattered lids, a desiccated mouth opened in a wide, silent scream, leathered cheeks stretched until they cracked.

"Daniel!" Jack grabbed his arm, turning him away from the window. He had a gun in his hand. "What happened?"

Daniel's voice was jammed, words stuck in his throat. "Outside…" he managed, lifting a shaking hand to point.

"What?" Jack looked at the window, night-black and empty. "You saw something?"

The panic was easing now, like a weight lifting, and he sucked in a breath. "Crap," he said, bending over, hands braced on his knees, catching his breath as the world started to spin. He felt like he'd sprinted a mile. "Crap…"

Jack's hand was on his back. "Easy," he said. Then, "Carter, go check on Gordon. Teal'c, you see anything out there?"

After a moment, "I do not, O'Neill."

"It was there," Daniel said, straightening up. He felt lightheaded, but better, less fogged in the head. "There was a face at the window."

"What kind of face?" Jack said.

He closed his eyes against the memory, against the horrific panic that had incapacitated him. Against the malevolence he'd seen in that spectral face. "A dead one," he said.

Jack gave his shoulder a reassuring squeeze, then let go with a sigh. "I was afraid you were gonna say that."

CHAPTER FOUR

"SIERRA Golf Charlie this is Sierra Golf One Niner, over."
Wait.

"Sierra Golf Charlie this is Sierra Golf One Niner, over."
Nothing.

"Sierra Golf Charlie this is Sierra Golf One Niner, over."

Teal'c let out a slow breath, allowed his mind to rise above the irritation simmering below. Anger was rarely useful unless in battle, and this was not a battle situation. He must use reason. "I do not believe you will be successful, O'Neill, no matter how often you repeat the exercise."

O'Neill glowered, then threw down the microphone and slumped back in his seat, rubbing his hands over his face. He appeared tired, as did they all; no one had slept after Daniel Jackson's encounter.

"Insanity," Dr. Gordon muttered, from where he lurked in the doorway that led back to his laboratory, "is doing the same thing over and over again and expecting different results — Einstein. And 'insanity' is an apposite descriptor of our current situation."

O'Neill allowed his hands to fall into his lap. "If you're gonna be an ass," he said, "be an ass someplace else."

"Need I remind you, Colonel, that *you* are the uninvited guest? Feel free to leave, by all means. We have a four wheel drive you can dig out — you'll reach Keflavik by the New Year, I'm sure."

"Don't tempt me," O'Neill growled, although Teal'c knew it was an empty threat. O'Neill would not leave this place when an unknown danger, possibly Goa'uld, had been loosed upon the world. "Teal'c," O'Neill said, "go check—"

"What did you call him?" Monroe said, from where he sat at the table.

A beat of silence fell. "Nickname," O'Neill said then, although Teal'c could see that he was irritated at his slipup. "It means—"

He was saved from further falsehoods by the door opening. Captain Carter had returned from her investigation of the antenna. She'd already shed her boots in the anteroom and was pulling her coat off as she stepped into the living area. "Sir," she said, "it's definitely the antenna."

"It came down in the storm?"

She shook her head. "Looks like it's been snapped in half, sir."

"Deliberately?"

She glanced around the room, at Dr. Gordon and Dr. Monroe, then returned her attention to O'Neill. "Looks that way, sir, yes."

"Dammit."

Gordon gave a huff of disapproval. "I suppose you're going to suggest that the walking corpse is responsible? That a three-thousand-year-old Norse warrior has come back from the dead and is sabotaging our radio equipment?" He snorted. "Farcical."

"Sir," Captain Carter said, perhaps sensing O'Neill's thinning patience and attempting to divert a confrontation, "I'd like to take another look at the chamber in the long barrow. The weather's definitely better today. I saw some stars out, so the clouds have cleared, and it'll be sunrise in a couple hours. I think we could leave now."

"How about it, Daniel?" O'Neill said. "Fancy a stroll?"

Daniel Jackson lay stretched out on the sofa, lost in thought. He had been pensive since the incident in the night and Teal'c wondered if he doubted what he had seen, or perhaps doubted himself. "Um, sure," Daniel Jackson said, as if surfacing from a dark place. "I'd like to take another look at the inscriptions in the burial chamber."

"I'm sure you would," Dr. Gordon said. "But don't for a moment think I'm going to let you in there unescorted."

"Well, feel free to tag along," O'Neill said, standing up. "It's probably best we stick together."

"Oh yes, of course, in case the walking corpse returns."

"I know what I saw," Daniel Jackson snapped. "I'm not making it up. I'm not crazy."

O'Neill gave him a warning look. "We know."

But Daniel Jackson just frowned, shaking his head as he climbed to his feet. "I'll get my stuff," he said. "I'd like to photograph the columns if I can."

As he disappeared toward the laboratory, O'Neill watched him go with obvious concern. He glanced at Teal'c, as he often did, silently seeking his opinion.

"It takes a great deal to disturb Daniel Jackson," Teal'c observed, keeping his voice for O'Neill's ears alone.

"Yeah," he said. "That's what's bothering me."

Carter was right, the weather had lifted and the sky on the western horizon was pinpricked with stars. To the east, a twilight glow had set in — prelude to the noonday dawn. The moon hadn't risen at all yet.

It was cold though, colder than during the storm. Ice crusted the surface of the new snow and Jack could feel his breath freezing on the fur lining of his hood. He was glad to be on skis and not on one of the snowmobiles. The exercise warmed his blood, even if it didn't blast away the lingering cobwebs in his head.

The sun was still below the horizon when they reached the site of the long barrow, but the clouds were turning golden and the pre-dawn light glistening on the snow was breathtaking. It was almost enough to make him forget why they were there. He pushed down his hood to take in the three-sixty view.

"Beautiful, isn't it?" Monroe said. He snatched his woolen cap off his head, scratched gloved fingers through his hair, then tugged the cap back down again. "Enough to inspire a hundred folktales."

"I just wish I had my camera."

"I'd love to come back here," Carter said, "under different circumstances."

And wouldn't that be nice?

"Jack?" Daniel interrupted his thoughts, calling from the door of the shelter. "I'm going to head down into the barrow."

"Not on your own," Jack warned. "Just wait a minute. Teal'c — don't let him go down there alone."

Teal'c nodded and strode into the building after Daniel, leaving Jack and Carter to unclip their skis.

"Stay and watch the sunrise," Monroe said after a moment. "It's a beautiful sight."

Jack was tempted to join him, even if the offer was mostly directed at Carter. And maybe in a different life he could have stood there and watched the sun rise without a care in the world. But not now, not in this life.

"We should go inside," Carter said, her eyes lingering on the golden horizon. Maybe she was thinking the same thing?

"Stay and watch, if you like, Captain," he said. "I'll keep an eye on Daniel."

She shook her head. "I'd rather get to work, sir. Maybe another time."

"Sure. Maybe another time." He took a breath of icy cold air and turned away from the sunrise. "Come on," he said, "let's go keep the archaeologists from killing each other."

After half an hour down in the dark, dank burial chamber Jack couldn't remember why he'd wanted to stop the archeologists from killing each other — Dr. Gordon, especially.

"I'll not let you take digital images of my discovery!" he was bleating. Again.

"You don't own it," Daniel sniped back. "You can't stop me. Now please move."

Across the room, Jack saw Teal'c shift impatiently. Carter, on the other hand, appeared oblivious. She had one of her scanning devices out and was crouched down, almost out of sight, behind the dais. Occasionally he heard her mutter something below her breath.

The flash of Daniel's camera went off once, twice, three times and left Jack blinking away red spots from in front of his eyes. "Daniel," he complained, "a little warning?"

"I demand copies of those images," Gordon carried on. "You have no right to publish anything based on —"

"I'm not publishing," Daniel snapped, moving on to the next pillar. "That's not what this is about."

Flash, flash. The next pillar done. More spots in front of Jack's eyes.

"Sir?" Carter's head popped up from behind the dais.

Jack pressed his fingers into his eyes, trying to dislodge the spots, and focused on Carter's face, pallid in the beam of his flashlight. "Whatcha got?" he said, heading over.

She threw a look at Gordon, but he was still busy harassing Daniel and was paying no attention. Even so, she beckoned Jack closer and he crouched down next to her. "Look," she said quietly, showing him the scanner. There was something pulsing in slow, regular intervals. "It's an energy signature," she explained. "From inside the dais."

"Asgard?"

Carter nodded. "It's very faint, though, almost a residue at this point."

"Any idea what it does?"

"There's a component missing," she said, "but I'm pretty sure it was generating some kind of containment or suppression field." She glanced again at Gordon, and lowered her voice further. "And if the body is what we think it is…"

Jack considered the idea. "So the Asgard stuck some Goa'uld in a containment field and buried them? Seems odd, don't you think?"

She made a face, half agreeing. "Maybe. But it fits the evidence."

"So what went wrong?" he said. "Batteries run out of juice?"

"No, I don't think so, sir." She stood up and shone her flashlight onto the dais, letting it dance across a hole at the head of the dark stone. "Like I said, there's something missing — the component that emitted the containment field, probably. Without it, the circuit's broken."

Jack glanced over at Gordon. "You think they took it?"

She shrugged and said, "It would have been a crystal — from the size of the hole it's roughly spherical, about ten centimeters in diameter." She glanced at him. "It would have looked like an enormous gemstone."

"So they took it and sleeping beauty woke up?"

"It's a theory."

At the moment, it was the only one. He scrubbed a hand through his hair. "We really need to find this snake."

"Yes sir."

From the other side of the chamber, there was a sudden scuffle. "How dare you? I will not be manhandled!"

Jack looked over and saw Teal'c, one hand on Gordon's shoulder, moving him away from Daniel. "You are interfering with work you do not understand," Teal'c said. "I will not permit it."

"You are in no position to permit or —"

A shout from up top startled them all. The room rang with sudden silence, all eyes focused on the black gap that led out of the long barrow. There was no other sound.

Jack stood up, reaching for the handgun under his coat. No one else moved. "Monroe?" he called.

"He won't hear you from in here," Gordon said.

He had a point. "Teal'c, with me. Carter, keep an eye on things down here."

"Jack?" Daniel was looking at him, white-faced in the dark. "Be careful."

By the time he was in the narrow passageway leading up to the surface, Jack had his Beretta in his hand. So did Teal'c. He signaled a stop at the bottom of the ladder that led up to the surface and they both stood and listened for a good minute. There was no sound but the wind whipping around the outside of the shelter.

"Stay close," Jack murmured to Teal'c and climbed the short ladder until he could see out into the shed. The door stood open and sunlight gleamed across the snow outside, low and pale gold. Dazzling. Inside, all was quiet. Moving silently, Jack climbed the rest of the way out and gestured for Teal'c to follow.

Slipping on his sunglasses, he moved to the door. Teal'c took the other side and they paused again, listening. Still nothing but the wind. On Jack's nod, they left the building at the same moment, back to back and weapons raised.

"Clear," Jack said. He could see nothing but snow and the distant mountains.

"There are footprints," Teal'c said.

Jack turned and looked where Teal'c was indicating. A trail of footprints in the snow led around to the far side of the shed. "Monroe," Jack guessed.

The sky was pale blue, the sun a ball of fire just above the horizon. The world had been transformed from the dark into something beautiful, and yet still Jack felt a sense of menace. A low buzz at the base of his neck. Danger.

He glanced at Teal'c. "You sensing anything?"

"I do not sense the presence of a Goa'uld," he said. "Yet I do sense *something*."

"Yeah," Jack agreed. "Something."

Keeping his weapon drawn and ready, Jack followed Monroe's footsteps around to the back of the shed. Maybe there was nothing wrong. Maybe the guy had cried out when he tripped on the ice. Maybe he was taking a pee. Maybe he'd tripped while taking a pee.

Or not. As they rounded the corner, Monroe's red coat was brazen against the snow as he crouched, looking at something on the ground. Jack stopped, glanced at Teal'c. He only lifted an eyebrow, but Jack interpreted it as, *Your call.*

Lowering his weapon, Jack said, "Hey, Monroe, whatcha got?"

He didn't respond.

Jack's finger moved to the trigger. "Hey, Monroe!"

He turned then, looking at them from behind his mirrored sunglasses.

"Found something?" Jack said, still not getting any closer.

Monroe nodded.

"What?" Jack stepped closer, but not too close, as Monroe stood up to reveal the body of a man lying in the snow. A very old, very dead man with the remains of a scraggy beard and a face that wouldn't look out of place in a museum. "Stay back," he warned Monroe. Keeping his weapon leveled on the corpse, he toggled the radio on his shoulder. "Carter, Daniel — get up here. We've found our dead guy."

It took an hour to get the body back inside the shed — Gordon, inevitably, insisting on 'preserving the integrity of the find.' Jack didn't blame him. The thing needed some preservation; it was starting to stink.

Daniel had taken one look at the corpse's face and turned almost as white as the snow, and then he'd left the shelter and gone to sit outside in the sunshine. Odd behavior for Daniel, but Jack didn't have time to handle it right away. The first thing he had to establish was whether the thing had ever had a snake in its head. And that was pretty difficult with Gordon fussing over the body like a mother hen and Monroe sitting there without taking his eyes of the corpse for a moment.

Carter hovered close to the door, glancing outside every so often, obviously worried about Daniel.

"Teal'c?" Jack said. "Let's take a walk."

They headed outside, gathering Carter along the way. Daniel was some distance off, sitting sideways on one of the snowmobiles and gazing out across the icy plateau toward the mountains. The wind stirred the fur around the edge of his hood, the sun glinting off his sunglasses.

"Hey," Jack said as they drew closer, "you okay?"

Daniel shrugged. "Yeah," he said. "I guess."

"You guess?"

He shook his head, frowned. "That thing…" He shuddered. "That was —" He lowered his voice, glancing back toward the shed. "I'm sure that's the face I saw at the window."

"I can see why it freaked you out," Carter said.

"Can you? I can't."

"Come on," Jack said. "Seeing that thing staring back at you in the middle of the night?"

"No, it was more than that." He still sounded freaked out, Jack realized. "I froze," Daniel said. "It totally paralyzed me. The fear, I mean. I've never felt anything like it. Never." He rubbed at the back of his neck, at the same spot Jack could feel a knot of tension tightening in his own neck. "And I can still feel it."

"I think we're all feeling a little strange," Carter said. "I know I am. Maybe it's the jetlag and the lack of normal daylight."

"Atmospheric pressure?" Daniel asked her, a ghost of a smile on his lips.

"Maybe not that."

Jack blew out a breath. "Okay," he said, "first things first. Teal'c, Carter — anyone sensing anything snaky?"

Carter glanced at Teal'c, as if looking for confirmation, then said, "No sir."

"I concur," Teal'c said. "If the body was possessed by a Goa'uld, it is no longer present."

"Which leaves the question, where did it go?"

"Perhaps it encountered another human?" Teal'c said. "It would certainly require a more…robust host."

Jack nodded and glanced back at the shed. "Monroe?"

"I do not believe so. I do not sense the presence of a Goa'uld."

"I'm not getting anything either, sir," Carter said.

Daniel pulled off his sunglasses, rubbed at his eyes. "You know," he said, "there is another option."

"Which is what?"

"That it isn't a Goa'uld at all." He spread his hands, defending the proposition before anyone could argue. "I didn't see its eyes glow."

"What else could it be?" Carter said.

Daniel shrugged. "The *draugr* were said to be bodies possessed by undead, unquiet spirits. Maybe it's something we haven't encountered before?"

"I don't believe in ghosts, Daniel," said Jack.

"Three years ago, you didn't believe in aliens."

"Not the same."

"Isn't it?"

Jack pulled off his watch cap, scratched his itchy head. He hated when Daniel did this, challenged what they thought they knew. "Look, whatever this thing is — or was — we need backup." He looked at Carter. "We need to get that radio working."

"Yes sir. I think I'll be able to fix the antenna if the weather holds." She glanced at the sun, still rolling along the horizon. "We've got a couple more hours of usable light too, if we head back now."

"Then do it. We'll —"

"Wait," Daniel said. "We can't just leave that thing here, unguarded."

Jack looked at him, trying to gauge how serious he was being. "Really? It looks pretty dead."

"It looked pretty dead last night. Standing at the kitchen window."

"Daniel…"

"It's evil, Jack. Don't ask me to explain. I can't. I can only tell you how it made me feel — how it still makes me feel. That thing…it's malevolent. We can't just leave it here."

Something cold ran down Jack's spine, despite the sunlight. There was just too much honest fear in Daniel's eyes to ignore.

"I will stay and stand guard tonight," Teal'c offered.

Jack nodded. "Yeah, not alone you won't."

"Sir —" Carter began, but he cut her off.

"You and Daniel head back to the camp," he said. "Take Monroe and Gordon with you. Get the radio working and brief the SGC. We've missed our last check-in, so they've probably contacted NASKEF by now."

"Yes sir." She threw an uncertain look at the shed. "You want me to bring over some provisions later?"

"Nah," he said. "I've got a couple of MREs in my pack. We'll be eating better than you guys."

Daniel shook his head, jumped down from the snowmobile. "Forget the MREs," he said. "Just make sure you've got plenty of ammunition."

CHAPTER FIVE

AS SOON as Daniel stepped into the cabin he could smell it: death. It was the same stench that had seeped from the ancient corpse. And that, in itself, was unusual. Wrong, even. Ancient corpses shouldn't smell like this.

"It must be on our clothes," Sam said, sniffing at the sleeve of her coat. "From when we were moving the body."

Daniel nodded because it was the only plausible explanation. But, then, what did plausibility have to do with their current situation?

"I need to fix the antenna," Sam sighed, with a dubious glance out the window at the fading daylight, "but then I'm taking a shower."

Pulling off his parka, Daniel threw it onto one of the chairs. The last thing he wanted to do was shower; he felt like he didn't dare turn his back on the world for a moment. "I don't like this place," he decided.

"No," Sam agreed. "It feels… I don't know, exactly. It feels…"

"Wrong?" Daniel supplied.

"Yeah. That's it. Everything feels wrong."

He sighed, suddenly weary. "Sorry," he said.

"For what?"

"For dragging you up here, spoiling your Christmas."

"You didn't — on either count."

"But still…" He gestured around the cluttered cabin,

the darkening windows. "I've had better Christmases."

"I've had worse," Sam said, then obviously forced a smile and gave Daniel a friendly punch on the shoulder. "Hey, at least we're spending it with friends, right?"

He shrugged in acknowledgement, but couldn't help throwing a look toward the lab, where Gordon and Monroe had disappeared. "Not only friends."

"Ignore them," Sam said. "They have no idea what's going on here."

"And we do?"

She smiled at that. "At least we understand the parameters."

"Doesn't exactly narrow it down," Daniel pointed out. The parameters were as wide as the galaxy.

Sam shrugged and pulled her hood up, preparing to go back outside and tinker with the antenna. "We'll figure it out," she assured him. "We just need some backup."

He wished he could be so certain. But Sam hadn't seen what he'd seen; she hadn't felt the incomprehensible terror that had drawn him toward the corpse even as it had repelled him. And Sam was an eternal optimist, a firm believer in understanding the universe in order to fix it. But what if not everything could be understood; what if not everything could be fixed?

As the door closed behind her, letting in a squall of icy air, Daniel turned back to the silent room. From the corner of his eye he could see the kitchen, the window a darkening square of glass behind the sink. He didn't look at it directly, could feel his heart pumping hard. He felt like his blood had been suffused with adrenaline all day, that his head was thumping with it. He needed to do something, to act, not sit around in this cramped little cabin.

He scrubbed fingers through his hair and wished he'd stayed behind with Jack and Teal'c. At least then he'd know where the thing was; he'd know it wouldn't appear at that damn window again. His fingers made fists in his hair and he found he couldn't breathe, his chest crushing tight in rising panic.

"Damn it," he hissed, just as he heard footsteps coming from the lab.

Embarrassed, he dropped his hands and looked up to see Monroe walking slowly into the kitchen. He was still wearing his coat, his woolen hat pulled down over his ears.

Daniel turned away, trying to drag himself back together. The last thing he wanted was the pompous academics to see him lose it. They already thought he was crazy and there was no need to confirm it. But he couldn't shake the panic, couldn't stop his heart thundering in his chest. What on earth was wrong with him?

Behind him he heard a cupboard open, the rustle of food packaging, the sound of Monroe eating. And still Daniel's skin crawled, making it impossible to stand still.

"I need to talk to Dr. Gordon," he blurted, heading toward the lab. It was just an excuse to move, to get out of there. To *do* something. Monroe didn't answer but Daniel didn't care.

It helped a little, getting away from the window's baleful glare, and Daniel always felt most at home in research labs, surrounded by the immutable artifacts of the past.

Dr. Gordon glanced up from the microscope he was peering through when Daniel entered, his hard face growing harder still when he realized who was invading his space. "What do *you* want?"

"You brought back some samples?" Daniel said. "From the body?"

"Naturally," Gordon said, and pushed shut his desk drawer with his foot.

"I don't suppose I could take a look?"

"No."

Daniel sighed. "Fine." At least he had photos of the Asgard inscriptions to work on. He didn't want to return to the living quarters, to the kitchen, so he found a chair as far from Gordon as possible and pulled out his camera. "Mind if I use your computer?" It would be easier to translate them if he could print the images.

Gordon didn't look up. "All my files are encrypted."

"I'm not interested in your files," Daniel said, and didn't explain any further. He was weary of the argument. He just wanted to do his job and go home. And since when had that ever been his attitude?

He shook his head and ejected the CompactFlash card from his camera. *This place*, he thought, *is driving me crazy.*

It wasn't as simple a job as Sam had hoped. Not only was the antenna itself broken, but the guy lines that had anchored it to the roof of the hut were gone and, without them, there was no way the antenna would stand up. Especially not in this kind of weather.

She pushed the hood of her coat back to peer up at the darkening sky. The sun was below the horizon now and its lingering twilight was being mopped up by heavy clouds. She could maybe take the pieces of antenna inside and figure out a way to strap them together, but mounting it back on the roof was going to be a problem without the guy lines.

Especially now that it was dark. Oh, and also snowing, she realized as a couple of thick flakes landed on her sleeve.

"Dammit," she growled, and kicked a clump of snow in frustration. She'd promised the colonel she could fix it. He was relying on her to call for backup. And now she was letting him down. She hated letting people down. "*Dammit*," she said again, with more vehemence.

She turned her face away from the wind, watching snowflakes fly past in the light from the cabin windows. She toggled her radio. "Colonel O'Neill, this is Carter. Over."

"O'Neill, go ahead Carter."

"Sir, I'm having trouble getting the radio working. Weather's closing in again, and I've lost too much light."

"Understood. Everything's quiet here, it can wait until morning."

"Yes sir. Sorry, sir." She winced; she hated apologizing too.

There was a pause, the radio equivalent of a sigh. *"You can only do what you can do, Carter. Check in at 1700 hours. Out."*

Disgruntled, Sam made her way back to the cabin, dragging the two long pieces of antenna behind her. How was it, she wondered, that she could fix a dozen different kinds of alien technology but a simple radio was defeating her? A radio and the weather.

She left her snowy boots and coat in the cloakroom, dripping with everyone else's gear, and padded in her socks into the living quarters. There was no one there, although the kitchen looked like it had been raided. And, back inside, she realized she could still smell the stink of the corpse. Perhaps it was in her hair? It was too short to actually sniff, but she figured a shower wouldn't go amiss. Maybe it would help her shake off the persistent tension building at the base of her skull too.

By dint of being the only woman in the cabin, she'd been given the guest quarters — a tiny room, just big enough for a cot bed, but complete with an *en suite* shower. She wasn't about to turn that down on any principle of equality.

With some relief she stripped out of her clothes and stepped into the small cubicle. The water was hot, even if space was limited, and she stood there beneath the water for a long time, just letting it flow over her. Letting her thoughts flow too.

She hadn't been lying when she told Daniel that she'd had worse Christmases than this, but if she was honest with herself it had been a long time since she'd had any kind of proper Christmas — the kind with family, friends, and loved ones around her. She supposed it was the price she had to pay for this life she led, and it wasn't so high. Not really. It was just that sometimes she wished…

She lifted her face to the water, let it run across her eyelids and wash away the regret. There were some thoughts it just wasn't worth thinking and she —

A thump. Something in her room had fallen to the floor. "Daniel?" she called, heart suddenly racing, but all she could hear was the hiss of the shower. She scrabbled to turn off the water and stood dripping in the sudden silence. "Daniel, is that you?"

There was no reply, but she thought she could hear movement. Was someone in her bedroom? Grabbing her towel, she wrapped it around her body and cursed herself, unreasonably, for not bringing her weapon into the bathroom. Pressing her ear against the door, she listened again but this time she heard nothing.

Water dripped from her hair, running down her face, dripping onto the floor. She swiped a hand across her face, and then grabbed the door handle. Taking a breath she prepared as best she could, given that she was wearing nothing but a towel, and flung open the bathroom door. It crashed against the wall, bouncing back with force, and she stuck out a hand to catch the rebounding door. The room was empty.

She went straight to the small drawer in the bedside cabinet. Her Beretta was still there. Her pack, though, lay on its side, the content spilling from the top. It had probably just fallen over. That's probably what she'd heard. Probably.

She shivered; it was cold in here, without the steam from the shower, and she was wet which made it worse. It stank too, she realized then. As the scent of shampoo dissipated, the stench returned. Death and decay. It wasn't in her hair, it was everywhere.

Sam pressed her face into her towel, and then rubbed it over her head to dry her hair.

This place, she thought, was driving her crazy. The sooner they got out of here the better.

It was cold in the shed that covered the site of the dig. The small heating unit lifted the temperature a little, but not enough for comfort and Teal'c was grateful for his heavy clothing — and for his symbiote, which was able to compensate for many of the effects of the cold.

He suspected that matters were worse for O'Neill,

who prowled the small space like an animal caged. Agile minds like O'Neill's rebelled against all kinds of restraint, even when entered into voluntarily, and Teal'c feared that this night would prove extremely taxing on them both.

"It is at times such as this," he observed at last, "when some knowledge of the art of kel'nor'reem would be of benefit, O'Neill."

"We're standing guard, Teal'c," he said. "Not snoozing."

Teal'c bristled. "Kel'no'reem is not 'snoozing'. It is a deliberate meditative state that enhances perception."

"Right, whatever. This is no time for yoga."

It appeared that O'Neill was in a belligerent mood. "Then it is a pity we cannot spar instead," Teal'c said, with enough menace in his voice to stop O'Neill's pacing.

"That bad, huh?" he said.

Teal'c did not believe the question required a reply.

O'Neill sighed and returned to where Teal'c sat on the workbench. "I feel antsy," he explained.

"I too feel ill at ease."

"Yeah?"

Teal'c glanced over at the corpse. It had remained inanimate since they had discovered it, and yet he viewed it with a disproportionate degree of distaste. "There is something unnatural about that…thing," he said.

O'Neill was silent, thinking. "It takes a lot to spook Daniel," he said after some time.

"You are not easily disturbed either," Teal'c pointed out. "Nor is Captain Carter."

"And yet…" O'Neill breathed a sigh of frustration. "Do you have *any* idea what's going on here?"

"I do not."

O'Neill's hand lifted to the radio on his shoulder then

fell away and he glanced at his watch. "I don't like splitting up," he said. "It's bad tactics."

"Not always."

"But still."

"Captain Carter and Daniel Jackson are well able to defend themselves, should the need arise."

O'Neill nodded, but said, "I've decided I don't like snow and ice. Bad things always happen on ice planets."

"We are not on an 'ice planet'," Teal'c pointed out.

"Principle's the same. Snow, ice — bad things."

"We have encountered dangers on many planets, with many different climates."

"You're missing the point," O'Neill grumbled and looked at his watch. "Close enough," he said, and toggled the button on his radio. "Carter, Daniel, this is O'Neill, over."

The reply came back instantly; Captain Carter had clearly been awaiting the check-in. *"Carter, go ahead, sir."*

"No news here, Captain. How about you?"

There was a pause, then, *"Everything seems quiet, sir. Over."*

Yet there was something tense in Captain Carter's voice, an uncertainty that Teal'c did not like.

O'Neill apparently noticed it too because he frowned. "You sure about that, Carter?"

"Yes sir. Just feeling edgy."

"Join the club."

There was a long static hiss, then *"...say again, sir? Over."*

"We're all on edge, Carter. Over."

This time, when O'Neill took his finger off the talk button, nothing came back. Teal'c felt a spike of tension and O'Neill resumed his pacing.

"Carter, respond." Nothing. "Daniel, this is O'Neill. Respond."

Nothing but static.

"Crap," O'Neill said, standing stock still in the middle of the shelter. "Now what?"

"It is probable that the adverse weather conditions are interfering with the signal."

"Probable," O'Neill growled. "Unless it's something else."

Teal'c shifted where he sat, his unease growing. He looked over at the corpse laid out in the far corner of the room. It had an evil aspect. Daniel Jackson had been right to describe its appearance as malevolent.

O'Neill paced the width of the shelter and back again, coming to a stop at the door. He put his palm on the wood, as if considering opening it. Outside the wind had grown stronger, new snow was falling.

"It would be foolish," Teal'c observed, "to attempt to return to the encampment tonight, in this weather."

"Yeah, I know." O'Neill sighed, pulled his hand from the door and instead rubbed the back of his neck. "Damn, but I hate this place. It's driving me crazy."

Within its pouch, his symbiote stirred uneasily and Teal'c could only concur with O'Neill's assessment. There was something very amiss about this place.

The tension was almost intolerable, drilling like a headache into the base of Sam's skull. Daniel felt it too, she could tell by the pallor of his face and the way he was rubbing his neck.

Gordon sat hunched over a meal at the end of the

table, eating rehydrated rice and beans without enthusiasm. But he was out of his lab, which was remarkable in itself. Monroe, on the other hand, was still working. On what, Sam didn't know and didn't really care.

It was silent, aside from the electrical buzz of kitchen appliances and Gordon's slow chewing. Sam wasn't hungry, though. All she really wanted to do was run, to get out of there and run and run and run…

She stood up, paced across to the window and stared out into the black. The dig site was too far away to see, but she couldn't help looking for a light. The radios had cut out a couple hours ago and she hadn't been able to raise either the colonel or Teal'c since.

The storm, she knew, had to be the reason. But still.

"Sam…?" Daniel didn't like it when she got close to the window. He sat with his back turned away from it, focusing on the images of the Asgard inscription that he was annotating. But he was looking up at her now, wary.

"There's nothing out there," she told him. "Nothing but more snow." Trapping her inside, trapping them all.

"You can't possibly be translating that," Gordon said then, as if he'd just noticed what Daniel was doing. He looked gray, his pinched face more acidic than usual. "That's an unknown alphabet."

"Unknown to you," Daniel said.

"And not to you? Be serious." Gordon pushed his food away as if it made him nauseous. "God, what is that stink?" he said, looking around him. "It smells like something died in here."

"It smells like that body you dug up," Sam said. "I think it got on our clothes or something when we moved it."

"Desiccated corpses don't smell," Daniel said. "At least, not like this."

Gordon took his plate into the kitchen, dumped the food. "He's right," he said. "This has nothing to do with my find."

Sam and Daniel exchanged a look. "I wouldn't be so sure about that," Daniel said, pushing it a little.

"Oh yes, I forgot," Gordon snapped. "It's an alien. Perhaps its flying saucer will come and beam it up?"

Daniel flung down his papers. "If you knew —"

"Daniel!" Sam cut him off, eyebrows lifted.

Gordon looked between them and spat out a laugh. "Absolutely farcical," he said, and not for the first time. "I'm going to bed. Do wake me up if the aliens invade, won't you?"

He stalked out and Daniel flung himself backward on the sofa, pressed his hands over his eyes. "Stupid, stupid, stupid."

"Yep," Sam said. "He is."

"I meant me," Daniel said, letting his hands fall, staring up at the ceiling.

Sam came to join him on the sofa. "You're tired," she said. "Everyone is."

Daniel turned his head toward her. "Are you worrying about Jack? And Teal'c?"

She nodded. "Are you?"

He looked back up at the ceiling. "I wish we could get them on the radio."

"It's the storm."

"You believe that?"

"Yeah," she said, because there was no reason not to, nothing but this sense of impending doom, of monsters in the dark. "What else could it be?"

Neither of them had an answer to that, at least not one they wanted to share. Sam stood up. "Get some sleep," she said. "I'll take the first watch."

Daniel didn't argue, which was testament to exactly how tired he was, and just stretched out on the shabby sofa. "I'll be right here," he said and didn't even take off his glasses when he closed his eyes.

Sam switched off a few lights, but left the light on above the stove. She didn't want to sit in the dark, listening to the wind howl. Her imagination was too powerful for that.

Despite his weariness, Daniel's sleep was plagued with dark, undefined dreams and when Sam put her hand on his arm to wake him he hardly felt like he'd closed his eyes. But the clock in the kitchen said two o'clock and Sam looked like she could barely keep her eyes open.

"Storm's died down," she said, but Daniel didn't follow her gesture toward the window. The last thing he wanted to do was look out into that lightless night. He shivered.

"Any contact from Jack and Teal'c?"

Sam shook her head. "I tried a couple times," she said. "Nothing."

In the darkness her eyes looked wide and fearful. He'd always thought her face was too expressive for a soldier; unlike with Jack and Teal'c, he always knew what Sam was feeling. "They'll be fine," he said, hoping it didn't sound trite.

Sam gave a quick nod. "Yeah," she said. "I know."

"Get some rest," he said, giving up the sofa to her.

He wanted coffee, but that black kitchen window was staring at him and he didn't dare get closer. Stupid, he knew, but the panic he'd felt last night was still hovering, like it was in his blood and waiting for the opportunity to rise. So, instead, he scrubbed a hand through his hair and went to sit at the kitchen table where the printouts of the Asgard inscriptions were waiting. He was making good progress on the translation, although so far it was mostly a lot of praise for the goddess Frejya. One thing was clear, however: the people who had built this long barrow had travelled far from their homes in order to bury the *draugr* far from their people. It was even possible that the Asgard — Frejya, he presumed — had beamed them here because there was a description of a white light that —

A door closed with a thump.

Daniel's head shot up, heart racing. There were footsteps coming from the direction of the lab, slow and deliberate, and with them Daniel felt panic stir in his blood. He found himself staring at the door that led from the living area back toward the lab, waiting for it to open.

The handle turned, the door creaked. Daniel's fingers curled around the pen he was holding as if it were a weapon. If only it were a weapon...

In the scant illumination cast by the stove light he watched as a figure appeared in the doorway. Daniel was frozen, unable to move. His head was thick with panic, his thoughts moving stickily. But then the man stepped further into the light, toward the kitchen, and Daniel recognized Monroe's red snow suit. He almost gasped in relief, sagging where he sat, watching the archaeologist head into the kitchen and open a cupboard.

It took a moment for Daniel's heart rate to decelerate, for the panic to recede — although it didn't go far, hovering nearby, ready to pounce. Perhaps that's why he didn't immediately register how odd it was that Monroe was still wearing his snow suit. That he still had his woolen hat drawn down over his ears. That he was standing in the kitchen eating dehydrated food directly from the packet...

Something was wrong.

Mouth dry, Daniel tried to swallow. Slowly, gripping the edge of the table, he rose to his feet. His body felt sluggish, as if it was resisting him, but he refused to be crippled by the fear battering the edges of his mind. Something was wrong here, and he had to find out what.

Monroe hadn't seen him, hidden as he was in the shadows, and Daniel moved closer with deliberate caution. There was a low kind of hissing noise that he realized was emanating from Monroe, a kind of monotone groan.

Daniel was about to speak, to ask him if he was okay, when he noticed the back of Monroe's hat. It was dark. It was dark with blood. He could see it now, in the yellow kitchen light. He could see blood on his neck and collar. Daniel tried to swallow, couldn't.

He was close, close enough to smell that same stench that had followed them back from the dig. With a sick feeling in the pit of his stomach, Daniel was beginning to realize who — or what — had brought it home. And there was only one way to find out.

His hand was shaking as he reached out, but that didn't stop him. He knew what he was looking for: the entry point in the back of the neck that would confirm what they were dealing with. He took a quick breath, snatched the hat from Monroe's head, and recoiled in horror.

There was no entry point. Instead, the back of the man's head was gone, caved in as if by a crushing blow. Not even a Goa'uld could have repaired so much damage to a host.

Monroe turned, slack-jawed, and fixed Daniel with a dead-eyed stare. Daniel had seen that stare before, looking back at him through the window. Whatever had once possessed the ancient corpse had somehow jumped into Monroe.

"Oh crap," Daniel breathed, backing up.

And then Monroe roared, a cry devoid of humanity, and charged at Daniel. He fended off the first blow, ducked the second. Monroe — or whatever the hell they were dealing with now — was clumsy, but he was also strong. And there was nowhere to go, the room was too small.

"Daniel!" Sam yelled from somewhere behind him. "Get down."

He dropped to the floor, heard her fire over his head. A single shot. A warning. "Back off!" she shouted.

Monroe kept on coming.

"It's not him!" Daniel said, scrabbling backward as the creature lumbered toward him.

Sam fired again, once, twice — chest and head. Blood bloomed, a fine mist of red. Daniel felt it on his face, saw it on his glasses. But the creature only stumbled back a step, before advancing again.

"What the hell is going on?" Gordon's voice, somewhere beyond Daniel's view.

"Lock yourself in the lab!" Sam barked at him.

"That's an order!" She fired again, one, two, into the creature. But it kept on coming.

"It's already dead!" Daniel realized, scrambling under the table and back to his feet. "You can't kill it!"

Which meant they were in a hell of a lot of trouble.

CHAPTER SIX

IT WAS too cold to sleep, which was lucky because sleeping was not top of Jack's agenda. He was too busy worrying about his team and second-guessing his decision to split them up.

The dead guy had done nothing but lay there, stinking. Meanwhile, Jack had no idea of half his team's status. He knew — logically — that they were fine. But he was a practical guy, and he liked evidence to support his logic. Until he made contact with Carter and Daniel, he was going to worry. It came with the job.

These people, this team… He'd served in close units before, but there was something about SG-1 that went beyond the usual bonds of loyalty and friendship. They were family, in a way. Not replacing the family he'd lost — that was impossible — but starting to fill the void left behind. Hammond might worry that the bonds were becoming too close, that Jack was compromising his objectivity, but Jack was convinced that, without that closeness, none of them would be able to handle the job they were doing, not if they wanted to hold on to their sanity. They were sharing things no one else in the world could understand. It was inevitable that they'd grow close, that his need to protect his people would feel this urgent, this visceral. He was their CO; it was his role to protect them. He wasn't crossing any lines.

He glanced over at Teal'c, who sat kel'no'reeming cross-legged on the counter. If he was worried about the others he wasn't letting on, but Jack knew that —

A gunshot, distant but clear.

Teal'c opened his eyes and for a moment they just stared at each other.

Two more measured shots from a Beretta.

"Crap," Jack hissed, and hit his radio. "Carter, Daniel — report."

Nothing but static, then another two gunshots.

Teal'c was on his feet. "We must assist them."

Jack wasn't arguing with that, pulling on his gloves and watch cap. "What the hell's going on over there?"

Teal'c didn't try to answer the impossible question, simply pulled on his own gloves and moved to the door. Outside the wind had dropped, but it was still snowing hard. "It will not be easy to return in darkness," Teal'c warned. "There is a danger we will become disoriented and lose our way."

"Yup," Jack said, grimacing at the blast of icy air. "Let's not do that."

Another gunshot rang out, and Jack felt it like a knot in the pit of his stomach. He wanted to be there, to help them, more than he wanted to draw his next breath. He reached for his skis at the exact moment something hit him, hard, on the back of his head and he fell face first into snowy oblivion.

"We have to drive it outside!" Sam yelled, reloading her weapon as the creature advanced.

It had its dead eyes on her, peering blankly through the bloody remains of its face. Perhaps she was the target because the gun made her the biggest threat? She could use that, she could work with that.

Walking backward, she lured the creature away from the table and toward the outside door. It gave Daniel enough time to dive for his pack and pull out his weapon. She heard him chamber a round.

"Hey!" he shouted at the creature. "Over here!"

It didn't respond, its attention fixed entirely on Sam. She felt her skin crawl, her heart racing with the unnatural panic the thing seemed to breed. Her palms were sweaty, but she kept the gun leveled.

A brief glance past the creature showed her Daniel, his weapon aimed at the back of the thing's head. He nodded, Sam dropped, and Daniel fired two shots in quick succession. The creature stumbled forward, roared a gasping, wet roar and turned back toward Daniel.

"Okay," he said, backing up. "Hello."

Sam was vaguely aware of Gordon, white-faced as he cowered close to the door leading back to the lab. He hadn't left, but there was nothing she could do about that now. She ran to the outside door, stuffed her feet into her unlaced boots. "Daniel! We have to get it outside!"

Daniel glanced at her, then back at the stumbling creature. "Don't go out there," he warned.

"No choice." She lifted her weapon. "Get down!"

He ducked, she shot, the creature turned back toward her. "Come on then!" she goaded it, backing up. "Let's go play in the snow."

The creature growled again, its slack jaw working as if it was trying to speak. She recoiled from the idea that Monroe might still be in there somehow, alive and aware.

Behind her, she felt for the door handle and opened it.

Biting air blasted into the hut, slicing through her clothes. No coat, no gloves, no hat. Crap. She figured she only had a couple minutes before the cold would impair her.

Daniel, weapon raised, followed as the creature stumbled toward the open door — toward Sam. She felt like bait. Pity they didn't have a trap to spring outside...

She stepped down into the snow, fingers aching on the handle of her gun. Damn, but it was cold.

The creature paused on the threshold, as if sniffing the snow, sensing the cold. Its head swiveled, jaw still working despite the gore.

"Come on!" Sam shouted again, backing away from the hut. Snow was falling hard, the doorway was already blurry.

And then the creature started running, charging toward her. She tried to dive out the way, but it was too fast. Plowing into her, it knocked her down into the snow and grabbed the weapon from her hand.

"Daniel!" she screamed as it pinned her there, raising the gun like a hammer above her head.

A bullet blasted right through the creature's head, the force knocking it forward. Using its momentum, Sam pitched the thing over her head and face first into the snow. Then Daniel was hauling her to her feet.

"Run!" he shouted. "Get inside!"

She snatched up her weapon and ran. They both did.

The ancient corpse stood over O'Neill's inert body, a hammer in its hand poised to deliver the killing blow.

Teal'c would die before he allowed that to happen.

He aimed his Tau'ri weapon, wishing fervently that he held his staff instead. "Do not move," he instructed the corpse. The irony of telling a dead man to be still was not lost on him, despite the situation.

However, the thing did not appear to hear him, lifting its weapon for a second blow. Teal'c fired, the bullet aimed at the corpse's hand. Its bones were fragile, its skin all-but disintegrated. The hammer, and the hand holding it, fell into the snow. The creature threw its head back as if to howl, but the sound it made was dry and dusty and barely audible over the moan of the wind. But it looked at Teal'c with such malevolence, with such murderous hatred in its desiccated face, that he took a step back. And then it launched itself at him, rotten teeth and fingers of bone reaching for his throat as if to tear it out like an animal. Teal'c fired again, but the bullet passed right through the thin corpse and did not halt it.

The creature was light, however, worn thin by age, and Teal'c grabbed it by its ratted leather clothes and hurled it away, sending it crashing against the side of the shelter. Even that did not stop it, though, and it crouched, growling by the wall, close to where the hammer had fallen.

O'Neill stirred then, groaning and drawing the creature's murderous attention once more.

In the space between heartbeats it sprang for the weapon, hauling back its arm to strike O'Neill. Teal'c moved, slamming into the creature, tearing the hammer from its hand and swinging it against the thing's head. The blow knocked it to the ground, but did not kill it; he feared nothing could kill this monstrosity. So Teal'c reached down and grabbed it, lifting it into the air and flinging it bodily back inside the shelter. Then he slammed shut the door and leaned his weight against it as the creature trapped inside threw itself against the door.

Catching his breath, Teal'c watched O'Neill push himself onto his hands and knees. There was blood in the snow.

"We have been attacked," Teal'c said. "You received a blow to the head."

"Yeah…" O'Neill's speech was slurred. "Where's the colonel?"

Teal'c felt a pulse of disquiet. "Do you remember where you are, O'Neill?"

"Gotta tell the colonel the charges are set," he said, sitting back on his heels. His face was ghastly in the thin light leaking past the edges of the door and there was blood running freely from his temple. "Gotta…oh crap." His eyes rolled back and he slumped sideways.

Across the ice came the echo of another gunshot.

Teal'c cursed, loudly.

Then, gathering his composure, he considered his position: it was not good. O'Neill required urgent medical attention, Captain Carter and Daniel Jackson were under attack by an unknown enemy while, behind him, a murderous and ancient corpse was throwing itself against the door. His options were limited.

But then his eye fell on the hammer the creature had used to attack O'Neill. It lay close to the creature's hand in the snow. Teal'c had an idea.

It was not difficult to use the hammer to wedge the handle so as to keep it from turning. Gingerly, he moved away from the door. He saw it shudder with another impact, but it did not open. It would not last for long, he knew, but at least it would give him a chance.

He crouched down next to O'Neill, pressed his fingers to his friend's neck. O'Neill's heartbeat was slow and faint, but at least it was there. Teal'c tapped his face. "O'Neill? O'Neill, you must wake up."

Nothing. Behind him, the assault on the door continued. The hammer shifted a little against the handle; he did not have long and he knew what he must do.

With some difficulty, Teal'c hauled O'Neill over his shoulder and began to run through the dark and the snow toward his friends and their unknown assailant.

They'd barricaded the door and pulled the storm shutters over the windows. Outside, they could still hear Monroe — what had once been Monroe — prowling around the hut, its howls louder than the howling wind.

Sam hovered close to the window, watching through a gap in the shutters, while Gordon sat on the sofa, ashen-faced and shaking. He hadn't said a word since Daniel and Sam had barreled back into the hut and slammed the door, only to find him crouched and immobile in the kitchen. He had that crazed thousand-yard stare with which Daniel was oh-so-familiar, and he might have felt some pity for the guy if he hadn't been such a colossal ass for the past three days.

"He's in shock," Sam said, noticing the direction of Daniel's gaze.

"Aren't we all?" He offered her a weary smile. "I don't suppose you have any idea what…?"

She shook her head. Her lips were still blue-tinged from her roll-around in the snow, but otherwise she looked okay. Well, as okay as he did, he supposed. Her fingers darted to the radio at her shoulder and away again and he saw the anxiety in her eyes. He shared it. They'd both heard the distant gunshots coming from the direction of the dig site and could guess what it meant.

"What I'm afraid of," Sam said at last, "is that we're looking at an infection, not a single organism like a Goa'uld."

Daniel nodded. "Because if the body back at the dig is still…" he struggled to find the right word.

"Animate?" Sam supplied.

"Right. If it's still animate then it must have infected Monroe somehow."

Sam held his eyes for a moment before she said, "Which means we might be infected too."

He remembered the spray of Monroe's blood on his face and felt his stomach turn. "That's… That's bad."

"Yeah."

He ran his fingers through his hair, glanced again at Gordon. He wasn't sure if he was listening, if he was even aware of where he was. "We should give him some tea," he said. "Or maybe they've got a shot of something?"

Sam nodded, visibly shaking off her grim thoughts. "Yeah," she said. "Yeah, good idea."

But she didn't move from her place by the window, and he could see from the distant look on her face that she was turning something over in her mind. He let her get on with it and started opening cupboards in the kitchen. It didn't take long to find a half-full bottle of vodka and he poured a generous shot into a scratched glass.

"Here," he said, offering it to Gordon as he sat down next to him on the sofa. "It'll take the edge off."

Gordon blinked and for a moment Daniel thought he'd refuse, but then he took the glass in a shaking hand and swallowed a mouthful. He shuddered, made a face, but after a moment breathed out a deep sigh and said, "Tell me this is a nightmare. I'm dreaming this."

"I'm afraid not," Daniel said, even as the thing outside howled again. Eager this time, although thankfully farther away from the hut.

Gordon wrapped both his hands around the glass, stared down into it, and said, "What…" He broke off, started again. "What happened to him? To Ed?"

Daniel glanced over at Sam who was peering out past the shutters again. He doubted she could see much, but understood her need to watch. "We don't know," he said.

"Not good enough," Gordon snapped. "That's not good enough."

"I'm telling you the truth. We've never seen anything like this before."

Gordon shook his head and when he looked up there was fury in his eyes. "I don't believe you," he said. "Something brought you here. You knew. You must have known something, or why else come? Why else bring soldiers here?"

From the window, Sam said, "Tell him, Daniel."

He blinked at her. "Tell him?"

She shrugged, but he could see a hint of a smile in her eyes — a little vicarious *schadenfreude*. "He's seen enough, he might as well know the truth."

Gordon looked at her, then back to Daniel. "So help me, if you try to tell me this has anything to do with little green men I'll—"

"They're gray, actually," Daniel said. "And they're about yea high."

"A man is dead, Jackson. Dead or… or I don't know what. How dare you sit here and—"

"They call themselves the Asgard," Daniel plowed on. "And they left a warning on the grave binding you found. I recognized the script because I'd seen it before, on… other sites. So I could translate it." He gave a humorless smile. "Basically, it said 'Do Not Enter on pain of a gruesome death'." He glanced at Sam, then back to Gordon. "I guess now we know why."

Gordon stared, his jaw working. "Good God," he said, "you actually believe this nonsense, don't you?"

"Because it's true," Sam said, turning her back on the window and folding her arms across her chest. "Whatever you uncovered, Dr. Gordon, had been trapped here three thousand years ago by an alien race whose technology far exceeds our current understanding. What we have to figure out now is what, exactly, you've unleashed on the world. And how we can contain it."

Daniel swallowed, but couldn't get rid of the sudden tightness in his throat. The men who had brought the ancient corpse here thousands of years ago had chosen a place far from civilization, but it wasn't so far removed now. If it was a contagion, some kind of disease…

"I wish I had a sample," Sam said, pacing toward the door and back. "Maybe I could try and figure out what we're dealing with if I could get it under a decent microscope?"

"Once we're in contact with the SGC," Daniel said, "they'll send a team. Dr. Fraiser will figure it out."

Sam nodded. "Maybe," she said, and cast a baleful look at the radio. "But that might be too late."

For us, were the unspoken words. Daniel sighed. "Look," he said, "we —"

A loud gunshot made them all jump. It was right outside. Sam flung open the shutters and Daniel jumped to his feet. "Turn off the light," Sam barked. "I can't see out."

He did so and she pressed her face to the glass, hands cupped around her eyes. "It's Teal'c."

Daniel didn't bother to look. He just grabbed his gun and moved to the door.

"Go to the lab," Sam barked at Gordon. "Stay there."

Whether Gordon complied, Daniel didn't know. He'd already shouldered open the door, his weapon raised. Teal'c was fifty yards out, turning in a slow 360, his gun raised and leveled. But he wasn't trying to run toward the cabin, he was just standing there. "Teal'c!" Daniel yelled, stepping down into the snow. "Come on!"

Behind him, Sam said, "Careful. We don't know where it is."

"No, I see it," Daniel said. There was a figure crouching in the snow; he could make out Monroe's red snowsuit. It was moving, dragging its leg as if it were injured, and circling Teal'c.

"We need to distract it," Sam said, stepped out of the cabin and shutting the door behind her. The light cut off, but the snow had stopped falling and there was a low moon ghosting behind thinning clouds. The night had turned silver and black. "I'll go — Wait," she said. "Where's the colonel?"

That's when Daniel saw the shape in the snow behind Teal'c and realized why Teal'c wasn't running. He was guarding something; he was guarding Jack. "He's down," he said through gritted teeth. "Jack's down."

"What? Where —? Damn it, I see him."

Teal'c was still turning, his focus intent. And then he stopped, facing them. "Captain Carter!" he shouted, just as something fell from the roof and knocked Daniel into the snow.

"Daniel!" Sam yelled.

He felt leathery hands about his neck and the noxious stench of death filled his lungs.

Horrified, disgusted, he bucked under the weight on his back and a moment later it was gone. He pushed back to his feet, only to see Sam wrestling with the monstrous corpse from the dig. Daniel gagged, on the smell and the horror, but he couldn't let it freeze him again. Not now.

Behind him, the thing that had been Monroe howled and he heard Teal'c's weapon discharge — for all the good that would do.

"Jackson!" The shout came from the door of the cabin. Gordon stood there with something in his hands. A can. "It's petrol."

Daniel ran over, staggering through the snow. "Yes," he said. "Good."

Sam had fought free of the creature — it was weaker than Monroe, its ancient body fragile. A hand was already missing and its arm was twisted. Sam was backing off, her weapon raised.

Daniel crouched in the snow, unscrewed the cap on the can. "Sam, wait."

She glanced. "Hurry."

He did, hefting the open can and flinging gasoline over the creature. "Now!" he yelled, and Sam fired.

The thing went up like a torch, roaring as it fell back into the snow.

Sam didn't wait to watch, she was already running toward Teal'c who was fighting off Monroe. Teal'c's face was bloody, but whether it was his own blood or

Monroe's, Daniel couldn't be sure.

"Teal'c, back off!" Sam shouted as Daniel reached her. He was trying not to slosh the gasoline as he ran.

Teal'c didn't go far. "I cannot leave O'Neill."

"Hey!" Sam yelled, firing into Monroe's leg. The thing staggered, turned, hissed through bloody lips. "Yeah, remember me?" she said, and backed up a step. Daniel kept pace with her as the creature moved away from Teal'c and Jack.

As soon as it turned away, Teal'c ducked, grabbed Jack under his arms, and started dragging him through the snow. Daniel tried not to be distracted by the boneless loll of Jack's head.

"Daniel, now," Sam hissed.

He flung the gas, Sam fired, and Monroe was wrapped in flames, thrashing and screaming.

Teal'c staggered toward them, exhausted, and Daniel ran to help. Between them, they hauled Jack upright and half ran the few yards back to the cabin. Gordon stood with the door wide, waiting for them, and Sam fell back to cover their retreat.

But the flames were already extinguished and in the silver darkness Daniel could see the creatures stirring. The night was far from over.

CHAPTER SEVEN

THEY LAY the colonel on the sofa, milk-faced in the fluorescent lighting of the cabin. There was a gash on the side of his head, and swelling. Sam bit back a curse and felt for the pulse in his neck.

"They're getting up," Daniel said, from where he stood at the window peering out into the night.

"How's that possible?" Gordon asked. "I saw them burn. How could they survive that?"

"Because they're not human anymore," Sam said, glancing up from the colonel. Gordon's face was bloodless, but at least he was functioning. "The bodies are just hosts to whatever has infected them."

He didn't answer that, his gaze dipping to the colonel. "We have some medical supplies," he offered.

Beneath her fingers, the colonel's pulse was fast and thready. "Thanks," she said, "but what he needs is a doctor."

"Ironic," Daniel said. "There are three doctors in here and none of us any use."

Sam almost smiled, but the sight of the colonel so helpless was profoundly disturbing and she found that she couldn't.

"Yep," Daniel continued after a moment, "it looks like they're communicating somehow. They're just standing there together."

"We must prepare for an assault," Teal'c said. "We must

barricade the door and windows."

"Yeah," Sam said. "See what you can find, Teal'c. Dr. Gordon — show him anything that might be of use. A hammer, nails. Anything."

"I'll go with them," Daniel said.

"No. Stay at the window. Keep those things in sight until —" Her hand was still on the colonel's shoulder, so she felt him stir and looked down to see him blinking in the harsh overhead light. "Colonel?"

He grimaced, made a clumsy attempt to shield his eyes.

"The light's too bright," Sam realized. A moment later, Daniel had switched it off and only the low light of a desk lamp lit the room.

She gave the colonel's face a gentle tap and he opened his eyes, face crunching into a scowl. He probably had the mother of all headaches. "Carter?"

"Yes sir." She felt a huge surge of relief; at least he knew who she was. "You took a blow to the head."

He lifted a hand, fingers fumbling over the dressing Teal'c had administered. "Ow," he said, managing to sound affronted.

"Sir, do you remember what happened?"

"Something hit me." That made her laugh a little, but it sounded more like tightly wound anxiety than amusement so she bit down on it hard.

And maybe the colonel saw that, or maybe he was remembering, because his frown deepened and he said, "We heard gunshots."

"We're okay, sir."

"Teal'c and Daniel?"

"Right here," Daniel said from the window. "Teal'c's barricading the door."

"Against *what*?" He tried to sit up but Sam pressed a hand to his chest, holding him in place.

"Stay there," she warned. "You're concussed."

He laid back and pressed the heels of his hands to his forehead. "Against what?" he repeated. "Gou'uld?"

"We don't know what they are," Daniel said. He pulled off his glasses and rubbed his eyes. "The body from the long barrow? It's animate, somehow."

"Animate?"

"That's what attacked you, sir," Carter said, shifting where she crouched at the colonel's side. "It's what Daniel saw last night, at the window."

"And whatever's animated the corpse," Daniel added, "also infected Monroe." He nodded toward the window. "They're both out there."

The colonel's mouth worked, like he was struggling to find the words. He probably was, she realized; who knew what damage a blow like that could have caused? "Us?" he said at last, looking to Sam for the answer. "Are we infected?"

But she had no answer to give. "I don't know, sir. Maybe."

He closed his eyes again and Sam was torn between keeping him awake and letting him rest, but after a moment he held out his hand and said, "Tylenol."

She sat back on her heels and frowned. "Sir…" Over the past couple of years she'd learned to put a great deal of meaning into that one, simple word. Right now it meant *I know what you're thinking, but there's no way you're getting up off that sofa.*

The colonel turned his head — she could see the waves of pain the movement caused flash across his face — and said, "Tylenol, Captain. Now."

She bristled at the order, but she couldn't refuse it. "Yes sir," she said, and didn't care that her tone bordered on insubordination; if any one of his team had suffered a head wound like this, he'd have ordered them to stay on the damn sofa. Irritably, she reached into her med kit for the Tylenol. "You'll have to sit up to swallow them," she said pointedly, because she knew exactly how much fun that would be.

The colonel's eyes narrowed but he didn't protest as he pushed himself upright. His stomach, however, did — just as she'd guessed it would. Luckily she was prepared and shoved a bowl into his hands just in time. After he'd thrown up, he swilled a mouthful of water around his mouth, spat it out, and then held out a defiant hand for the Tylenol.

Sam just shook her head, unsure whether his mulishness was admirable or foolish. Both, probably. "You have a severe concussion," she warned him as she handed over the pills. "You should rest."

"Sure," he said with a pasty smile. "Later."

"You're risking permanent brain damage, sir."

"It's okay," he said, swallowing the pills. "No one will notice."

Tight lipped, she reached into her med kit and pulled out a syringe. "At least let me give you a Phenergan shot," she said. "For the nausea."

"Nice try, Carter." He half smiled because, obviously, he knew it was also a sedative. "How about you give me a sitrep instead?"

With a sigh she had to admit defeat, dropped the Phenergan back into her medkit, and gave him the report he wanted. It didn't take long to fill him in on what she knew — which wasn't a great deal — and he listened with his eyes closed, head resting on the back of the sofa. He was still, pasty looking, and she wondered if he was listening or whether his injury was getting the better of him. But as soon as she stopped talking he said, "So it's an infection, then? Some kind of disease?"

"I think so," she said.

Outside a sudden, unnatural howling rose up. "They're coming closer," Daniel said, his face pressed to the window. "They're heading for the cabin."

"Crap," the colonel said, and reached for his weapon.

"I gave your gun to Teal'c," she told him.

He didn't comment on that, just said, "What's plan B, Carter?"

"I figure there'll be a chopper out from Keflavik later today, sir," she said. "General Hammond would have alerted them when we didn't check in yesterday and the weather's clear enough now that they can fly."

"Problem is," Daniel said, "we can't let them land."

"Not if we're infected," the colonel agreed.

With a frustrated sigh, Sam got to her feet. "Which we won't know for sure until we can get a blood sample back to the SGC."

The colonel lifted a hand, gestured toward her. "That's not your blood, right?"

She touched her face. "What? Oh. No, it's…" She grimaced at the thought. "It's probably Monroe's."

"Can you use it?" the colonel said. "Test it, somehow?"

"Me? I could try, sir," she said, although she wasn't confident. "There's a basic optical microscope in the lab, but I don't know if it'll be anywhere near powerful enough. And as far as labs go, it's pretty basic. They don't even have a centrifuge, so I couldn't fractionate the blood. Plus, I don't have any idea what to look for." She sighed. "We really need Dr. Fraiser."

"We don't need Fraiser," the colonel said. "We've got you. Now go figure out what this is, Captain."

For a moment she just looked at him, considering what he was asking. He always had so much faith in her, but this time he was literally asking the impossible. "I'm sorry, sir," she said at last, "but I can't do it."

"Carter —"

"With all due respect, Colonel, what you're asking isn't possible. I don't have the equipment or the expertise."

His eyebrows rose. "Then improvise. It's what you do best."

"Actually," she said, "there may be an alternative." She threw a glance at Daniel to see if he'd agreed. "We don't actually need to know what this is because we already know how to contain it."

"Carter," the colonel sighed, "I have the mother of all headaches. Don't be cryptic."

"Sorry sir. I mean the Asgard device in the long barrow. Whatever this is, they designed that device to contain it. Right, Daniel?"

"Um, yes," he said. "That's certainly what the Asgard narrative implies. Frejya — the goddess — bound the *draugr* in its grave to keep it from plaguing the village of **Helgatofta**."

"So," Sam said, "all we need to do is get the device working again." She hesitated, thinking it through. "And, of course, we need to lure both Monroe and the Norse corpse down into the long barrow…"

"Oh," the colonel said, "is that all?"

Sam smiled at his wry tone. "Sir, trust me, I stand a better chance of fixing the Asgard device than I do of figuring out how to cure this thing."

"But what about the missing component? Don't tell me you have a spare in your back pocket."

Sam shook her head and glanced over the colonel's shoulder toward the archeologists' lab. "But I think we both know where it is."

Daniel turned away from the window, his face somber in the lamplight. "Uh, Sam?" he said. "I hate to say it, but if we're infected too…?"

The question hung in the silence between them for several heartbeats. Then the colonel said, "We quarantine ourselves as well. At least the SGC will know where to find us when Fraiser comes up with a cure."

Sam quailed at the thought of trapping themselves inside the long barrow with Monroe and the ancient corpse, but she knew they had no choice. And, despite the colonel's optimism, she couldn't help but wonder why, if this contagion could be cured, the Asgard hadn't cured it three thousand years ago.

"Okay," Daniel said, clapping his hands and rubbing them together briskly. "So who volunteers to tell Dr. Gordon the plan?"

"Absolutely not! Are you insane? Going back there is suicide. You might as well shoot me in the head and be done with it."

"That can be arranged," Jack growled. The pain in his head was intense, and his patience — what he had of it — was paper thin. It didn't help that Carter had been watching him with sharp, disapproving eyes since he's levered himself onto his feet.

"Look," Daniel said, hands raised as if he were talking to one of the truculent locals they usually dealt with. Which, Jack supposed, was exactly what he was doing. "I know you're frightened, we all are, but this is our best chance of ending this. Just tell me if you have the crystal."

Gordon had retreated to the rear of the laboratory and stood with his back to the bench, arms folded across his chest. "Our best chance of surviving this is to stay here and wait for rescue."

Daniel shook his head. "We can't do that; we can't risk spreading the infection."

"Is that what this is, then? A disease?" Gordon's eyes narrowed his panic receding for a moment. "Did you bring this here? Is this some kind of CIA experiment gone wrong?"

Jack glanced at Carter. *CIA?* Where had *that* come from?

She gave a shrug. "It's not a conspiracy," she told Gordon. "We told you the truth. And we need you to do the same. If you have that crystal, then there's a good chance I can get the device in the long barrow working again."

"If you think I believe that alien nonsense, then you've got another thing coming," he said, but as he spoke his gaze darted sideways toward his desk drawer.

"Look," Jack said, "I don't really care what you believe. But you are going to tell us what you've done with the damn crystal. That's not a request, it's an order."

"You can't give me orders." But again his gaze moved to his desk, and this time so did Carter.

"Hey!" Gordon spluttered, darting forward as Carter

pulled opened the drawer and started rummaging. "Stop that! How dare you —"

Jack put himself between Carter and the archeologist, a hand on his chest. "Uh-uh. Stay there."

"Don't you touch me. Don' t you —"

A sudden thump against the back wall made them all jump. Gordon's pallid skin turned ashen. "See?" he said. "You *see* what's out there?"

Another thump, this one close to the window behind Gordon. He turned, panicked. "Oh God," he hissed, "they're trying to get in."

Jack felt a squirming sense of panic in the pit of his stomach. He was used to fear, used to adrenalin, but this was different. This felt alien, other — imposed on him. He reached for his weapon, but it wasn't there. "Damn it," he hissed.

"O'Neill," said Teal'c, and held his gun out to him.

Jack took it with relief, but the weight of it in his hand only settled his panic by a fraction. He chambered a round and squeezed his eyes shut for a moment against the thundering pain in his head. He felt nauseous. He felt like a liability.

"Got it!" Carter's exclamation hit like a bolt of relief. He glanced over his shoulder, saw a baseball sized crystal in her hand, glittering under the strip lighting, and in that split second of relief Gordon pushed past him and made a lunge for the crystal.

"Give it to me!" he cried.

Jack tried to shoulder him out of the way, but his reactions were impaired, he was too slow, and he ended up pushing Gordon into Carter. Gordon's flailing arm knocked the crystal right out of her hand and, in a horrible suspended moment that was still too fast to stop, he watched the crystal sail through the air and shatter on the floor.

"You idiot!" Carter shoved Gordon back so hard he fell on his ass. Then she was on her knees, picking up the crystal shards and shoving them into her vest.

Outside, the hammering was becoming louder, more insistent. Jack felt as if it was inside his skull, each thump resonating through his head. He squeezed his eyes shut; it didn't help.

"Carter," he said, backing away a step.

She scrambled to her feet at his side. "I got most of it, sir, there might me a way to —"

"Carter," he said again, because his vision was starting to blur. "Your orders are to get everyone — including me — into the long barrow and to activate the device. Contact the SGC if you can and initiate Protocol 303."

Carter's face remained as shuttered as the windows, tight lipped with worry. "Sir?"

"Head injury," he said, by way of explanation.

Her answering nod was curt. "Just stay on your feet until we get there, sir."

Glass shattered, scattering out from behind the shutter with a howl of wind and blast of icy air. Gordon screamed, stumbled back.

"We're going," Carter barked. "Get to the door."

"NO!" Gordon whirled on them, stark panic in his eyes. "I won't go out there again!"

Jack felt his vision slur, double, return to normal. He staggered sideways and that's when Gordon grabbed for his weapon. Jack swung for him, but he was dizzy and it went wide and cost him his balance. He fell and felt the gun slip from his fingers.

"Jack!" Daniel was at his side, holding him up, and when he opened his eyes he saw Gordon holding his weapon, aiming it with shaking hands at Carter. Her gun was raised too, steady as a rock, and aimed right back at him.

"Okay," Daniel said. "Just take it easy."

He stood up with care, leaving Jack slumped on the floor, concentrating on not throwing up again. He could feel icy air on his face, on his hands, sinking to the floor as it crept in past the broken window. The scrabble of bony fingers on the shutters made his skin crawl with that strange and alien panic.

"I won't go out there," Gordon said. "I won't do it."

"Okay," Daniel said. "I understand. You're frightened."

Jack looked up, managed to focus on Teal'c who stood to Gordon's left. Teal'c's brief answering nod told Jack that he already knew what to do.

"The thing is," Daniel said, keeping up his unwitting distraction, "we need to consider all the options —"

Teal'c moved, lunging for the weapon Gordon was holding. But pumped on adrenaline and terror, Gordon was faster than he looked. Wrenching the gun out of the way, he fired. The shot went high, up into the ceiling, sending everyone diving for cover.

Gordon backed away another step. "Get away from me!" he yelled. "Don't come near me."

"Dr. Gordon," Daniel said. "This isn't the way to —"

Turning wildly, he fired again and only missed Daniel by a fraction. "I won't go out there!"

Outside the creatures were howling, clawing at the window. Jack could see their fingers working loose the shutters. He had to get his people out. He had to get them out now.

If he'd had a weapon, he'd have taken the shot himself, but he could see Teal'c on the far side of Gordon. He'd taken cover around the corner leading back to the living area. Jack gave the signal to fire.

"Stand down," Teal'c said, moving out from behind his cover with his pistol aimed. "Or I will fire."

Just then, the shutter fell away from the window. It clattered to the floor and through the shattered glass Jack got his first look at Monroe — what Monroe had become. His face was burned and twisted and his bloody fingers scrabbled blindly at the window frame, driven by something more than sight. Behind him, the corpse from the dig howled into the night, sending a verifiable chill down Jack's spine.

It was them, Jack realized, something about their presence that fueled the panic he was feeling. It pressed in at the back of his skull, in competition with the pain already squeezing like a band around his head.

Something about them was making them all crazy.

Especially Gordon. He let out a scream, inarticulate and wild, and fired at the thing that had been his friend.

"Teal'c!" Jack shouted. "Now!"

Teal'c's shot was precise, aimed at Gordon's right leg. It felled him, but somehow he kept hold of his weapon and swung it around, opening fire on Teal'c. There was blood, Teal'c fell backward, around the corner and out of sight.

"Carter!" Jack yelled.

Gordon whirled at the sound of his voice and fired again. Jack ducked, heard a second shot, and when he looked up Gordon was sprawled on his back with a single shot through his head.

He glanced over his shoulder and saw Carter lower her weapon, her expression bleak.

"Nicely done," he said and tried to stand up. But the world tipped sideways and if Carter hadn't grabbed hold of him, he'd have fallen. "Damn it," he growled. His vision was starting to gray around the edges.

"Daniel!" Carter shouted. "Get Teal'c, get to the snowmobiles!"

The corpse was climbing in through the kitchen window, reeking of death and panic. "We have to get out," he said.

"Working on it, sir. You need to stay awake. You need to walk."

He did, stumbling like a drunk with his arm around her shoulder and her arm tight around his waist. Behind him he heard gunfire.

"It's Teal'c," Carter said. "He's okay."

And then they were outside and the cold slapped him in the face. It helped, helped keep him focused and aware.

"This way," Carter said.

He could see Daniel running ahead and then Teal'c was at his side. "I will assist O'Neill," he said.

"You're injured," Carter objected.

"It is minor."

The roar of an engine. "That one's ready to go," Daniel shouted, darting over to the second machine and kicking it into life.

"Not gonna be driving," Jack warned as the blood started to rush in his ears. He could feel consciousness slipping away.

Carter swore and the next thing he knew there was snow in his face and the wind was whipping the hood from his head. A huge pair of arms, one on either side of him, gripped the handlebars of the snowmobile and the engine thrummed beneath him. He tried to lift his head.

"Do not move, O'Neill."

He decided that was good advice and gave way to the icy darkness.

CHAPTER EIGHT

IN THE moonlight it was bright enough to see and in other circumstances the ride to the dig would have been fun — beautiful, even, beneath a sky full of diamond stars and the snow glistening like silver.

But Daniel was all too aware of the creatures in pursuit and of the impossible task ahead of them. He glanced back over his shoulder, felt Sam adjust her steering as his weight shifted. He figured they had an hour, maybe less, before the creatures pursuing them reached the dig.

They started to decelerate and Daniel turned around in time to see Teal'c and Jack cut in front of them as they approached the shelter covering the long barrow. Jack at least looked conscious.

"How is he?" Sam asked as soon as she'd killed the engine.

"He's fine, thanks for asking," Jack said, although he looked decidedly unsteady as he climbed off the snow-mobile. "I need to get one of these things," he said, giving the handlebars an appreciative pat.

"You don't have one?" Sam sounded surprised.

"You do?"

"Of course, sir."

Jack's reply was cut short by a howl from behind them, closer than Daniel expected.

Sam's expression tensed. "Let's get inside."

The generator was still running and lights were still on, which was a point in their favor. While Daniel closed the door — no windows here, at least — Sam and Teal'c dug out the flashlights. Jack just sat on the floor with his back to the wall and shut his eyes. He looked ghastly, in all senses of the word.

"I'm going down there," Sam announced, holding a flashlight.

"I will accompany you," said Teal'c.

"Nope." Jack opened an eye. "I need you and Daniel to hold the door, T. I'll go with Carter."

"Sir," Sam protested. "I think—"

"I can hold the damn flashlight," he said, climbing to his feet, one hand braced on the wall. "I'm no use up here."

No one could argue with that, least of all Sam. She just nodded and led the way down into the long barrow. Daniel watched them go until the bouncing beam of her flashlight was out of sight, then he turned back to Teal'c. "I hope this works."

Teal'c just lifted an eyebrow. "Indeed."

"I figure we've got forty-five minutes before Bert and Ernie show up."

Sam had already figured the same so she just said, "You should rest, sir."

He made a sound, something like a laugh, as he leaned back against the inert control panel and rested the flashlight on the floor between his knees. "Is that a polite way of telling me to shut up, Carter?"

"It's a polite way of telling you to rest, sir. Even thinking can hinder your recovery from a concussion."

"Well, you know I always leave the thinking to you."

"Hmm," she said, because they both knew that wasn't true.

She'd already pulled all the fragments of the crystal she'd salvaged out of her vest pocket and laid them on top of the dais. Looking at them lying there, broken and inert, it was difficult not to feel angry at Dr. Gordon. "This should have been easy," she muttered.

A beat fell before the colonel said, "Even easier if Gordon hadn't removed the thing in the first place. Or if he'd followed Daniel's instructions and stayed the hell outa here. Or if the Asgard had just zapped this Norse guy three-thousand years ago, instead of leaving him here for us to dig up."

Sam felt the colonel's gaze on her and looked up.

"Lots of 'ifs'," he said, making his point. "None of this is your fault. You had to take the shot."

She shrugged, because fault was immaterial. Gordon had died by her hand and she'd have to make peace with that in the end. But not now; now she had more important things to worry about.

Picking up a couple of the largest pieces of crystal, she slotted them together like a jigsaw puzzle. Was there a way, she wondered, of using what remained of the crystal to generate the containment field?

"Duct tape?" the colonel suggested.

It was enough to provoke a small smile. "I don't think that's going to cut it, sir."

"No," he said, touching a hand to the dressing she'd taped over his wound. He was probably bleeding again but she pushed that thought out of her mind.

Moving to the end of the dais, she inserted the longest piece of crystal into the slot, simply to see what happened. It just about bridged the gap and, to her surprise, flared with a sudden bright heat. Yanking it out before it could overload and shatter, she dropped the shard onto the dais and blew on her singed fingers. "Ow!"

The colonel looked like he was about to get up and look so she waved him away with her good hand. "It's okay, sir. Looks like we have power, at least."

"No kidding," he said, indicating the control panel he was leaning against. "This whole thing lit up like a Christmas tree."

Sam nodded. "Only problem is, there's too much power for what's left of the crystal." She prodded at the cooling chunk on the dais. "It'll shatter if it overloads. But if I could calibrate the power output to the size of the crystal then there's a chance it might generate a small containment field. Obviously the size of field would be relative to the size of the remaining emitter crystal but..." She looked around the chamber, at the columns full of Asgard runes, and wondered how large the original field had been.

"But?" the colonel prompted.

She shrugged. "I guess we'll see how big the field is once I get it working. But it could get cozy in here."

"Couple of candles," he said, "a little mood music. It'll be nice."

Sam swallowed her smile and returned her attention to the crystals. Colonel O'Neill, she'd discovered recently, was rather good at making her smile.

"You don't think we should keep the door closed?" Daniel said, peering over Teal'c's shoulder and out into the night.

"If I did," Teal'c said, "it would be closed."

Fair enough, Daniel supposed. Except that it was freezing and the little heat provided by the space heater was fleeing through the half-open door faster than it was being pumped out. He sighed and bounced on his toes to keep his blood flowing. "Can you see them?"

Teal'c's silence was his only answer.

"Okay, I get it. If you'd seen them, you'd have told me."

"I would."

Daniel glanced back at the opening to the long barrow, a black rectangle cut into the earth. It would be warmer down there, of course, but nevertheless it was a grave and tonight its true purpose was starker than ever before; if all went according to plan, they could all be interred inside by dawn. Buried alive. Or half-alive. Or half-dead, depending on your view of the world.

"I wonder how Sam's doing," he said. "Maybe I should —"

"Daniel Jackson," Teal'c said. "I see them."

His stomach gave a lurch. "Both of them?"

Teal'c paused before he said, "There are three figures approaching."

"Three?" Daniel pushed past him, opening the door wider so he could get a better look. Sure enough, there were three figures walking across the moonlit snow. They were still too far away to make out details, but Daniel recognized the limping, leg-dragging gait of Monroe. A taller figure, maybe the ancient Norseman, staggered along behind, but who was that striding out ahead?

There was only one possibility. "It's Gordon."

With a thump, Teal'c closed the door. "Matters are worse."

"Yeah." Daniel glanced around the shed, his eyes falling on the generator. "Let's use this to barricade the door."

Teal'c nodded, but said, "It will not hold them long."

"I know. But it only needs to hold them for long enough." He toggled his radio. "Sam, this is Daniel. Company's on the way. ETA a couple minutes."

A hiss of static, then, "I need ten."

He shared a look with Teal'c, who'd already unholstered his weapon. "We'll do what we can," he said and let his hand fall to his side. "Once more unto the breach, dear friend?"

Teal'c raised an eyebrow. "On Chulak we would say: *Arik tree-ac te kek*. It means —"

"No surrender, even in death."

"That is correct."

Outside Daniel could hear their enemies' approach — the shuffling groaning sound they made, the scuffing of feet in the freezing snow. "I guess death didn't stop these guys," he said to Teal'c. "Why should it stop us?"

Teal'c gave a small smile. "Spoken like a true warrior, my friend."

Daniel had to laugh at that, but his laugh was cut short by the first thump of a body against the door. He reached for his weapon and glanced at his watch. "Ten minutes," he said and started counting.

Through the pounding in his head, Jack could hear the attack begin, the noise funneling down through the narrow tunnel. No gunshots yet, but the dull reverberation of someone — something — pounding on the wooden shelter. It wouldn't be long before they were inside; the shelter was rudimentary, definitely not as strong as the cabin.

"Carter?" he said. She crouched next to him, studying the crystal array in the panel he was leaning against. "I don't want to rush you, but…"

"I know, sir." She didn't so much as glance at him as she spoke, her attention entirely focused on the array. "I just need to identify how the power output is regulated."

"Great," he said, "but Daniel and Teal'c will be down here soon and they're bringing guests."

"I *know*, sir."

There was a crash from above, a screech of wood and a shout that sounded like Daniel. "Crap," Jack said and pushed himself to his feet, ignoring the way the world was spinning.

"Sir?"

He waved away her concern. "Just get that thing working, Carter."

He still had his gun, at least, although he wasn't sure he trusted his aim right now. He could barely walk in a straight line, let alone fire in one.

"Jack?" Daniel's breathless voice came over the radio. "We're falling back."

He cursed under his breath, but into the radio he only said, "Copy that, I'll cover you."

Another chirp of radio static, then, "Jack, there's three of them. Gordon's been infected too."

Carter looked up. "But he was dead."

"They're all dead, Carter."

She shook her head. "No. I mean he was dead before he was infected. The infection didn't kill him — I did."

Jack just looked at her. Maybe it was the fog in his head, but he wasn't following her logic. "And the difference is?"

She scrubbed fingers through her hair and thought for a moment. "Daniel saw the back of Monroe's head; he said it was caved in, like it'd been smashed." Her gaze darted to his own head wound. "Maybe that's how this thing works," she said. "Maybe it uses corpses as hosts, and when it can't find any it makes its own."

Jack repressed a shudder at the thought of being next in line, that he might have become one of those shambling creatures — might have hurt his people. "That's just supposition, Carter."

"Yes sir. But if I'm right, then maybe this thing can only infect the dead."

"So we might be okay."

She gave an uncertain shrug. "As long as we don't die."

Jack glanced at the dark opening leading back to the surface. He could hear the fight coming closer and moved around the dais, his weapon held low and ready for use. "I wasn't planning on letting that happen, Captain," he said. "Now get that gizmo working so we can all go home."

There was no life in Gordon's eyes, but somehow there was that same malevolent intelligence Daniel had first sensed in the body of the Norseman. Intelligence and violence. And he felt the same suffocating panic, it was radiating from Gordon like heat.

Daniel stumbled back a step, his leaden legs difficult to move as the thing that had been Gordon lunged across the remains of the generator that still blocked the door. Teal'c fired, the impact knocking Gordon back. But not far. Not far enough to ease the terror.

"It's a weapon," Daniel realized, pressing his hands to his head and forcing himself to think through the panic.

"It's how they disable victims."

Teal'c was at his side and spared Daniel a brief look. "You refer to the sense of unease these creatures provoke?"

Unease? Try blind panic. But he didn't have time to discuss it; Monroe and the Norseman were pushing through the door now, their burned and bloody faces hideous, almost unrecognizable as human. Daniel's stomach rolled, he tasted bile.

Then Teal'c was in front of him, standing between him and the creatures. "Retreat," he ordered. "We cannot hold them in a space this large, but in the passageway below they can only attack one at a time."

And we can only defend one at a time, Daniel thought as he climbed on shaking legs down the ladder and into the frozen earth. It felt like he was climbing into his own grave. In fact, he was.

"*Teal'c, Daniel,*" Jack's voice barked over the radio. "*Report.*"

"We're in the tunnel," Daniel said, backing up so that Teal'c could follow. Only he didn't. "Teal'c?" He craned his head, looking back up into the light. He could see Teal'c's legs, braced, heard the report of his gun. Once, twice.

"Daniel Jackson, you must retreat!"

For a frozen moment he didn't move, he simply stood there, strung between blind panic and duty. He took a deep breath, rasping and cold. Then another. Behind him he heard movement, saw the beam of a flashlight on the wall ahead of him. Jack. Jack was coming, wounded as he was. Sam was still fixing the device.

And maybe that was what broke the spell. Simply knowing he had his team around him — his family — that he couldn't give in, couldn't let them down.

"Daniel Jackson!" Teal'c yelled again. "Go."

He shook his head, even though no one could see it. "No," he said beneath his breath. Then louder, "No."

He darted halfway up the ladder, braced his arms against the ground to steady his aim. He could see the things prowling around Teal'c, keeping their distance. Gordon's face was streaming blood, but the gunshot wounds didn't stop him any more than they stopped the others. It only ever slowed them down.

"Teal'c," he said, just loud enough to be heard, "you take Gordon and Monroe, I'll take the corpse. Then we both retreat."

"That is not a wise strategy."

"Maybe not," Daniel said. "But we retreat together or we both stay here. Your choice."

Teal'c muttered a curse that he probably thought Daniel couldn't translate. Then he said, "Very well. On the count of three. One, two —"

Daniel fired, so did Teal'c. The creatures howled and Daniel half-slid, half-fell down the ladder and stumbled back to make room for Teal'c. "Now, come on!"

"Hey, watch out!" Jack was behind him, one hand braced on the wall and the other holding his Beretta. Daniel didn't need to see his face to know that he probably shouldn't be on his feet.

Teal'c jumped down into the tunnel, but kept his weapon trained on the hole above him. "They are coming," he said, backing up a step. "We must move."

"Slowly," Jack said. "Carter needs more time."

But she didn't have it. Gordon had already leaped down into the passage, landing in a crouch. He hissed, vocalizing even if the creature had no discernible language. Jack lifted and fired his weapon in one swift motion, but the shot went wide and only clipped Gordon's shoulder.

"Dammit," Jack growled and Daniel saw him press a hand to the back of his neck.

The panic felt like pressure inside his skull and Daniel squeezed shut his eyes. "It's not real," he said. "They cause it, they use it to confuse their prey."

"Move!" Teal'c shouted, backing up as Gordon flew at him.

And then they were fighting in the dirt and Monroe was scrambling down the ladder, the Norseman right behind.

"Carter!" Jack shouted over his shoulder, back down the passageway. "You've got two minutes and we're coming in hot!"

Two minutes.

It was impossible, in two minutes.

Gunfire ricocheted along the narrow passageway, the sound thundering toward her. She could hear the colonel shouting orders, the creatures snarling. And in front of her all she could see was the crystal array and the transformer she was improvising from the innards of her radio. If she didn't step down the power output it would blow the remaining shards of crystal and then they'd be up the creek without any kind of paddle.

Another gunshot, this time closer.

She glanced over her shoulder, saw the colonel crouched in the doorway. There was movement beyond him, the sounds of a struggle. They were fighting hand-to-hand, resisting every step of the way, and Sam was out of time.

"Carter." The colonel's voice was taut. "Now would be good."

She didn't reply; she was too busy working.

"Daniel, go left," the colonel ordered.

In her mind's eye, Sam could see them pulling back into the chamber, forming a rough skirmisher line. Teal'c would be in the center, Daniel to the left, the colonel to the right. But he was injured and there were three of the creatures now. One-to-one: even odds, except that the creatures couldn't die and her team very much could.

She wrapped the last of her scavenged wiring around one of the power crystals and hoped it would do the job, but she was trying to mesh Asgard technology with kindergarten electronics and the chances weren't great.

"Carter!"

"Yes sir!" She moved away from the array, back to the dais where the crystal shards lay. She snatched up the largest and held it ready to insert into the emitter. If it worked, if the crystal didn't blow out, then it should create a small containment field. How large, she couldn't say. What would happen to her, trapped inside it with the creatures, she couldn't say either. But the rest of her team would be safe. She hoped.

Glancing up she could see the creatures now, the Norseman clambering into the chamber from the tunnel to join the other two. Her gaze skittered away from the sight of Gordon, the bullet hole she'd put in his forehead livid and unnatural as he stalked the colonel. They weren't attacking though, just biding their time, pressing her team back. They had the upper hand and they knew it.

"Colonel," she called, "you need to get out of their way — I need them to come closer to me."

"Carter —"

"Sir, they have to be inside the field when I activate it and I don't know how big it will be."

He bit off a curse, but gave the order. "Daniel, Teal'c — let them through."

Daniel was limping and Teal'c was bloodied as they pulled back to the left, taking cover behind the columns and leaving the colonel to go right, opening up a direct route for the creatures to reach Sam.

She felt it as they drew nearer, that sickening unease she'd experienced around Monroe. It made it difficult to remember what she was doing, why she was standing there letting these things stalk her. In her hand, the shard of crystal began to shake. It took a moment before she realized it was because she was trembling.

"Sam." Daniel's voice was distant but adamant. "It's them, they're doing it. They're making you feel like that. You're not really afraid."

Like interference, she thought. Static over the airwaves. She tried to tune it out.

Tearing her gaze away from the creatures, she saw Daniel watching her from the shadows of the columns, his weapon — for all the good it would do — trained on the Norseman. Teal'c was further behind, closer to the entry. She couldn't see the colonel.

She tightened her hold on the crystal. "Come on then," she said in a low voice. "Come and get me."

She didn't know if they understood her. There was no humanity left the things that were hunting them, but there was intelligence. A dark, malignant intelligence.

The creatures stopped moving, their heads turning as if listening.

"They're communicating," Daniel said. "I saw them do this before, outside the hut."

Communicating. Infections don't communicate, not like this. "Daniel," she said, "I think —"

But it was too late; they were moving. Gordon lunged for her first and she ducked out of his reach. Monroe and the Norseman were flanking her, but weren't close enough to the emitter yet.

"Sam, just do it!" Daniel shouted.

Whites of the eyes, Captain. She backed up a step. *Whites of the eyes.*

"Carter!" O'Neill barked from off to her right. "Now!"

She glanced in his direction and saw Monroe lumbering in fast. She flung herself toward the dais, but was too slow. A dead hand caught the back of her jacket, hauling her backward. She jabbed hard with her elbow, felt it connect with flesh and blood. Monroe stumbled, his balance lost momentarily. She used the slim advantage, slammed her elbow back again and twisted free of his grip.

But the Norseman was crouched on the dais now, snapping and hissing, and something was snatching at her ankle. She stumbled away from Monroe, right into the grip of the ancient corpse. Its stench, its leathery skin, revolted her but she ignored it and reached for the emitter with the hand holding the crystal. She was an inch short.

The Norseman had a fistful of her hair, yanking her back. The crystal slipped in her cold grasp. And then someone else was there and the creature holding her shrieked and let go, falling sideways. The colonel, his Beretta raised like a club, looked down at her.

"Do it," he said.

She scrambled over the dais and pressed the shard into place. For a moment nothing happened and all she could hear was her own harsh breathing.

But then the crystal began to pulse, not blazing as it had done earlier, but a soft steady glow. She stared at it, breathing hard.

"Sam," Daniel said, "look." The two columns nearest to the dais were glowing, the Asgard runes flickering as if made of fire. Some of the other pillars were flickering further back in the chamber, but there wasn't enough power to illuminate them all. And something was happening to the creatures too, they were staggering, their limbs twitching. Climbing off the dais, Sam backed away.

The colonel did the same. "Is it working?"

The Norseman was the first to fall, collapsing into a pile of old bones. Then Monroe and Gordon followed a moment later, sprawled across the dais.

Sam barked a relieved laugh. "Yes sir," she said, "I think it's working."

She glanced at him, at his ashen face and the livid wound on the side of his head. "Sweet," he said.

"I see no force shield," Teal'c said, coming to join them. His shoulder was bleeding where Gordon had shot him and there were scratch wounds on his face and neck from his fight with the creatures. But otherwise, he looked okay. Alive.

"I don't think it's that kind of containment field,"

Sam said, looking back at the bodies of the men. She took a step closer, lifted her hand to the symbols on the pillar. The light flickered orange across her skin but otherwise had no effect. "And I don't think it's an infection, not one we'd recognize."

"Then what is it?" Daniel said.

"I think it's some kind of life form."

"So are bacteria."

She shook her head. "No, I mean intelligent life. You saw how they were communicating. I think —"

"Um, Carter?"

The colonel was looking at something behind them. Sam turned, startled to see a woman standing there watching them. She was tall and wore a long dark cloak that shimmered and shifted as she moved. It was made entirely out of feathers.

"Oh," said Daniel. "Hello."

"*Velkomin*," the woman said, and bowed her head. "*Ek heiti Valfreyja...*"

"Yes," Daniel said, "I thought I recognized you. My name is Daniel and —"

But the woman continued talking as if Daniel hadn't spoken, and it was only when something rippled across the surface of her skin that Sam realized they were looking at a projection.

Daniel took a step closer as the woman continued to speak in her strange, lilting accent. "Fascinating," he said, examining her closely. "Absolutely fascinating. This is — Wow." He glanced over his shoulder at the rest of them. "This is actually the goddess Freyja."

"What's she saying?" the colonel said.

"Oh." Daniel turned back to the hologram. "Um,

she's welcoming us and she's telling us…" He listened more closely. "…that we're great warriors for having brought the *draugr* here, that the evil within it can't be destroyed but that she has used her power to bind it within its grave."

"This must be the recording played to the people who first brought the Norse warrior here," Sam realized. "It probably rebooted when I reinstalled the emitter crystal."

"Right," Daniel said, eyes bright with excitement, "which makes this an actual vision of the goddess Freyja. This could have informed the very origin of Norse mythology — in fact it *must have* inspired the sagas and the *Poetic Edda*! Look at the cloak of feathers — this is literally a living myth. I mean, think about it —"

"Daniel." The colonel was swaying, his face ashen and fingers tight around the grip of his weapon. "Anything tactical I need to know?"

"Oh, right," Daniel turned back to the hologram. "Okay… She says the *draugr* will stay here past the midnight sun and the midday night. Ah, that means all summer and all winter — so forever, essentially."

"Until curious archaeologists remove essential components of the device," Sam grumbled.

Daniel cocked his head, still listening. "Oh, now she's saying 'On this eve of Jól I bid you make merry and celebrate the rebirth of Sol, the light of the world.'"

The woman spread her arms, her feathered cloak spread like wings, and then the image was gone and the chamber was left in silence.

Daniel cleared his throat. "Um," he said, "I think she just wished us Happy Holidays.'"

"Okay," the colonel said, "then I'm done."

With that his eyes rolled, his legs gave way, and Sam only just caught him before his head cracked on the stone floor.

CHAPTER NINE

THERE'S pain in his head, people shouting over the noise of chopper blades. Controlled chaos. Is he being rescued, he wonders, or left behind?

But there's wind-blown snow in his face, not sand. And there's cold, not heat. This isn't Iraq.

"Colonel, can you hear me?" Someone shines a bright light into one eye, then the next. "Pupils are reactive," the same person says. He doesn't recognize the voice.

"We all need to be quarantined," someone else is saying, barking orders above her pay grade. Carter, it's Captain Carter.

"Major," she says, "Colonel Calvin needs to contact General Hammond immediately. He needs to tell him to initiate Protocol 303."

"Take it easy, Captain. First thing is to evac Colonel O'Neill back to Kef."

"Sir, he needs to be quarantined."

"He needs a doctor."

"One of us should go with him." Jack knows that voice; it's Daniel.

"You go," Carter says. "Teal'c and I will stay here until the SGC team arrives."

And then there's movement — he's being lifted on a stretcher — and when he manages to open his eyes he sees a deep blue sky above the whirling chopper blades.

Daniel's hand is on his shoulder when the helo lifts away from the ground. "It's okay, Jack," he says. "You're going to be okay."

He decides to believe him.

"Colonel, what do you think you're doing?"

Janet Fraiser stood, arms folded, in the doorway of the isolation room and Jack stopped with one leg in his BDU pants. "Don't you ever knock?"

"No," she said, apparently unfazed by his state of undress. "Why are you out of bed?"

He sat back down, trying to move carefully without looking like he was moving carefully. Fraiser didn't need to know exactly how woozy he still felt. "I heard Carter and Teal'c were back," he said, which was explanation enough. But Fraiser appeared unmoved, so he added, "Come on, doc, I've been stuck in here forever. And you said I'm not infectious…"

"Apparently not," she agreed, as if she wasn't entirely pleased about it. "But you do have a fractured skull. You need to rest."

"I'm too bored to rest."

And that was the truth. Four days in isolation, even with a head injury, was enough to test his patience. He didn't do well without distraction, his thoughts tended toward dark paths that led to times and places best forgotten. And since reading and TV were apparently banned too, it didn't leave a lot to occupy his mind. Even sleeping was risky when his thoughts were left to wander.

Maybe Fraiser saw something of that in his face — she knew his past better than anyone on base — because her expression softened a fraction.

"I'd rather you had a chair."

"Yeah," he said, "not a chance in hell."

She shook her head. "It's that or nothing, Colonel."

He held her stubborn gaze for as long as he could, but she wasn't giving way and his head hurt too much to win this battle through force of will. He waved a hand at her. "Fine," he said, "have it your way."

With a satisfied nod, she turned around. "I'll send a nurse with a wheelchair."

"Sure," he said.

Two minutes after she'd left, he was dressed and out the door. He figured Carter and Teal'c would be in the infirmary for their post-mission physicals, so he headed in that direction, keeping one hand braced on the wall to compensate for the irritating wobbliness in his legs.

But it was good to be up, good to be walking. Although he did feel rather more like a limp dishrag than he'd expected and he suspected he was walking kinda slow.

"Colonel?" A nurse paused to look at him with concern. "Does Dr. Fraiser know you're up?"

"Sure," he said. "Where're Captain Carter and Teal'c?"

"In the infirmary, sir," he said. "Do you need some help?"

"No, I'm fine." Jack dared him to disagree. "Why?"

Wisely, the kid backed down. "No reason, Colonel. Uh, Merry Christmas, sir."

Jack blinked at him. "Is it?"

"Sir?"

"Is it Christmas today?"

"Yes, sir."

"Huh," he said. "Well, Merry Christmas, Lieutenant." Strange, but saying the words didn't hurt quite a much as they usually did. His head on the other hand...

Fortunately the infirmary wasn't much further and he could hear Carter's voice before he pushed open the door. The sound made him smile.

She was sitting on one of the beds, talking to Fraiser, while Teal'c lay on the cot opposite, having the gunshot wound in his shoulder redressed. They both looked tired, but well.

"They're still working up the samples we took from the victims in Iceland," Fraiser was saying as Jack pushed open the door. "But it's unlike anything I've seen before. The closest comparator would be a virus, if a virus was able to work in cooperation with other viruses."

"Like insects?" Carter suggested. "A collective life form?"

"Right," Fraiser agreed. "They appear to colonize necrotic tissue but, rather than feeding on it as you'd expect, they utilize the existing neuro-pathways as a guide to replicating them in order to access the functions of the host."

Carter nodded as if the idea of alien insects taking up residence in dead humans made perfect sense. "And then they use the host bodies to find more suitable hosts."

"Or to make them, if they can't find them."

Carter looked thoughtful, scrubbed a hand over her tired face. "But they were intelligent," she said. "The creatures. The hosts."

Jack had to agree — it was difficult to forget the intelligence he'd sensed in the things that had attacked them — but Fraiser didn't sound convinced.

"In the way that a hive mind is intelligent, perhaps," she hedged. "But it exists only to feed, to reproduce, and to create more of itself. I doubt they're capable of complex thought."

"They could definitely communicate," Sam persisted. "We saw them."

The doc spread her hands. Clearly she wasn't going to argue the point. "Like I said, we're still researching. Whatever it is you found out there, Sam, one thing I can tell you for sure is that it's an entirely new life form."

"Extraterrestrial?"

"I can't answer that," Fraiser said. "But it's certainly unique, so far as I know."

Which didn't say much, given the size of the galaxy and the very tiny proportion of it they'd explored in the two years the Stargate program had been active.

"What I don't get," Carter said, "is why the Asgard just buried the host there. Why not beam it off the planet or destroy it?"

"Oh, Daniel has a theory about that," Fraiser said. "Ask him, if you've got a spare couple hours. It's something to do with his theory about Asgard principles of cultural preservation."

Carter smiled and pushed herself to her feet. "Actually," she said, "if I'm done I'd like to check in with Colonel O'Neill. How is he?"

"He's fine," Jack said from the door.

Carter smiled when she saw him. Fraiser scowled.

From his bed Teal'c said, "You do not appear to be 'fine', O'Neill."

"That's because he isn't fine," Fraiser said and pointed

to the bed Carter had just vacated. "Colonel, lie down. Now."

When he didn't argue, Fraiser raised a knowing eyebrow that clearly said 'I told you so'. Jack made no comment. He figured his ready compliance with doctor's orders was admission enough that he may have overestimated his level of recovery.

"So," he said, while a couple nurses fussed around with pillows behind his head, "what did I miss?"

Perched on the end of his bed, Carter, with occasional help from Teal'c, filled him on everything that Hammond hadn't already told him: how the deaths of the two archeologists had been explained to the Icelandic authorities, and how a team from Area 51 was on site at the long barrow, trying to find a more permanent fix to the Asgard device so that they could move the whole kit and caboodle back to Nevada. What the Icelandic government was being told, Carter wasn't sure, but that was Hammond's bailiwick. All Jack needed to know was that the threat had been neutralized and his team was home safe.

Carter trailed off when she reached the end of her report, glanced over at Teal'c and then back at Jack. "I guess I should let you guys get some rest," she said, with enough reluctance to make it obvious that she didn't particularly want to leave.

Which suited Jack, because he didn't particularly want her to go. "Hey," he said, "you know what day it is today?"

She looked at him blankly. "Friday?"

"Christmas," he said.

Her eyes widened. "Oh. Merry Christmas, sir."

"Yeah." He glanced around the infirmary. "They could have bought a tree, don't you think?"

"No tree," a familiar voice said from the doorway. "But I did bring pizza and ice cream."

Daniel, smiling behind his glasses and a flop of too-long hair, stood there with his arms full of takeout. "There's some kind of turkey dinner in the commissary," he said, "but since we're actually allowed to leave the base at last I thought I'd, you know, actually leave the base."

Carter's face split into a grin. "Daniel," she said, "I officially love you."

"Well." He smiled. "Then it was worth battling I-95 in the snow."

Jack smiled and, to hide exactly how much he was feeling, said, "Did you bring beer?"

Fraiser lifted her head where she was working on the far side of the infirmary, ready to object.

He held up a hand, forestalling the protest. "Okay, no beer."

Not that it mattered. What mattered was that SG-1 was home, alive, and more or less in one piece. What mattered was that Daniel and Carter were laughing, that Teal'c was almost smiling, and that Jack, sitting in the infirmary with a fractured skull, nibbling on slightly cold pizza, was having a better Christmas than he could have imagined. The first Christmas he'd had anything to celebrate in over four years.

Daniel lifted his glass — of water — in a toast. "To friends," he said, and after a moment added, "To family."

Jack could drink to that.

About the author

Sally Malcolm is the co-founder and commissioning editor of Fandemonium Books which has been publishing licensed novels based on the Stargate franchise since 2004.

In addition to commissioning and editing over fifty Stargate titles, Sally has also written several Stargate novels herself: *Stargate SG-1: A Matter of Honor*, *Stargate SG-1: The Cost of Honor* and *Stargate Atlantis: Rising* (novelization). With Laura Harper, she has co-written *Stargate SG-1: Hostile Ground*, *Stargate SG-1: Exile*, and *Stargate SG-1: Sunrise* (writing as J.F. Crane).

She has also penned four audio dramas for Big Finish Productions: "Stargate SG-1: Gift of the Gods" starring Michael Shanks, "Stargate Atlantis: Savarna" starring Teryl Rothery, "Stargate Atlantis: Perchance to Dream" starring Paul McGillion, and "Stargate SG-1: An Eye for an Eye" starring Michael Shanks, Claudia Black and Cliff Simon. Sally also wrote two episodes of the video game "Stargate SG-1 Unleashed" which were voiced by Richard Dean Anderson, Michael Shanks, Amanda Tapping and Chris Judge.

Her historical romance, *The Legend of the Gypsy Hawk*, is the first of the Pirates of Ile Sainte Anne series for Choc Lit UK and was published in January 2016.

Sally is currently working with Laura Harper on *Stargate SG-1: Insurrection*, the final book in the Apocalypse trilogy, due for publication in autumn 2016.

She lives in London with her American husband and two children.

STARGÅTE
SG·1.

STARGATE
ATLÅNTIS

Original novels based on the hit TV shows STARGATE SG-1 and STARGATE ATLANTIS

Available as e-books from leading online retailers

Paperback editions available from Amazon and IngramSpark

If you liked this book, please tell your friends and leave a review on a bookstore website. Thanks!

www.ingramcontent.com/pod-product-compliance
Lightning Source LLC
Chambersburg PA
CBHW011202190726
48286CB00009B/2882